CHRISTIE WILLIAMS
Haven River Rescue

Copyright © 2024 by Christie Williams

All rights reserved. No part of this publication may be reproduced, stored or transmitted in any form or by any means, electronic, mechanical, photocopying, recording, scanning, or otherwise without written permission from the publisher. It is illegal to copy this book, post it to a website, or distribute it by any other means without permission.

This novel is entirely a work of fiction. The names, characters and incidents portrayed in it are the work of the author's imagination. Any resemblance to actual persons, living or dead, events or localities is entirely coincidental.

Copyright 2024 Eliza Prokopovits

First edition

This book was professionally typeset on Reedsy. Find out more at reedsy.com

"It always protects, always trusts,
always hopes, always perseveres.
Love never fails."

                1 Corinthians 13: 7-8a

Contents

Acknowledgments	ii
Chapter 1	1
Chapter 2	8
Chapter 3	14
Chapter 4	23
Chapter 5	28
Chapter 6	41
Chapter 7	49
Chapter 8	61
Chapter 9	71
Chapter 10	82
Chapter 11	93
Chapter 12	102
Chapter 13	110
Chapter 14	123
Chapter 15	138
Chapter 16	152
Chapter 17	162
Chapter 18	170

Acknowledgments

A few words of thanks:

To my family, friends, and everyone who has supported me and cheered me on, thank you.

To Aly, for always being my enthusiastic first reader and for the gorgeous maps, you're the best.

To God, my King and Savior, for the words and inspiration—I couldn't have done it without You. I hope it brings You glory.

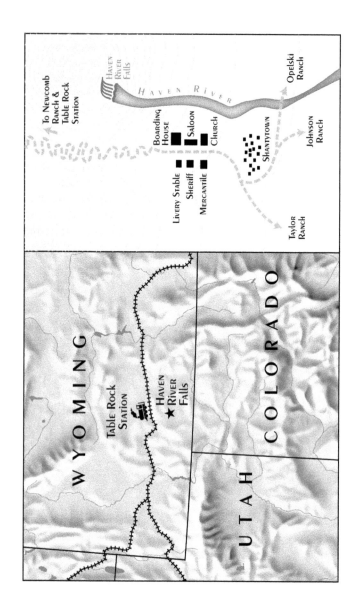

Chapter 1

Pennsylvania, July, 1880

Laurie stepped into her father's dim office and was struck by how different it looked. She'd only been avoiding it for... well, it had been a few months. The room hadn't changed a bit, but with the curtains closed and the desk tidy, it was unfamiliar, completely lacking its usual light and warmth, despite the July heat.

She forced herself to take a step inside, to cross to the window and open the curtain. Bright sunlight splashed across the oak desk in the center of the room. Pa had managed all the farm paperwork here, sitting in that chair with wire-rimmed glasses perched on his nose and his graying hair unkempt from all the times he ran his hands through it. He'd always looked up at Laurie with a smile when she knocked. She was never an interruption, more of a welcome distraction. When he was out working the farm, she'd come sit in his chair to do the household accounts, and somehow it used to give her the same sense of comfort and home that she'd had as a very small child when he'd hold her on his lap in the evening and tell her a story.

Now she turned her back on the desk and the chair and the conspicuous absence of her favorite person in the world.

The office didn't have much for furniture, but there was a small bookshelf on the wall between the windows, which held the family Bible, a few favorite novels, and the ever-present Farmer's Almanac. Laurie pulled two books from the shelf—her father's favorite, *Tom Sawyer*, and her mother's, *Sense and Sensibility*. Her mother had been a romantic at heart, though she was practical enough in day-to-day life. Laurie preferred the Twain book, but she couldn't part with either one. Tucking the books under one arm, she lovingly ran her fingers down the spine of the family Bible. She paused as footsteps in the hall came to a stop at the door and a throat cleared.

"You don't have to go, you know," Harvey said. "You can stay with us as long as you need. Mary would never want to force you from your own home."

Laurie hugged the books to her chest and turned to face her cousin. His brow was creased in a frown under his tousled sandy hair, and his nose had a touch of sunburn. "I know."

"Frankly, I think she'd like having you around to help her settle into running this place. You've done well with it for the past six years, and she admires that. We both do."

Laurie had taken over running the house after Mama died of a fever. It hadn't been easy for a thirteen-year-old to step into a grown woman's job, but she'd managed. "She won't want me around forever. She'll want to step into her rightful role of lady of the house, and it will be awkward for everyone if I'm still here."

She stifled a sigh. This was only another reiteration of a conversation she and Harvey had had dozens of times in the last weeks. Harvey and Mary had postponed their wedding an appropriate amount of time after Pa's death for mourning, but tomorrow was finally the day. Laurie had gone to school

CHAPTER 1

with Mary and had always thought she was a sweet girl, though that hadn't stopped Laurie from mercilessly teasing Harvey—who was more like an older brother than a cousin—when she noticed how lovesick he got around the girl. She was truly happy for them. They'd known all their lives that Harvey would inherit the farm, and Laurie had known that she would one day leave it, but the reality still took her breath sometimes.

"Besides," she said, "what difference will a week or a month or a year make? Staying only postpones the inevitable."

"You don't know that."

"Yes, I do. I have no marriage prospects here—all the men are either too old or too young. I'll be in Mary's way once she gets her bearings. And I don't want to be the maiden aunt who splits her time between helping with your children and raising goats." She made a face. "Much as I love it here, I don't belong anymore."

"But you enjoy raising goats."

Laurie couldn't help smiling. "I do. But that's not enough of a life, and you know it."

"So you're really going to stay with Beth and Esther?"

Laurie nodded. "Did you talk to Mr. Martin?"

Harvey shoved his hands into his pockets and nodded. "They agreed to buy your goats and offered to drive you to Harrisburg later this week. Said they're overdue for a visit anyway. They'll pay you for the goats when they pick you up."

"Thank you."

Harvey lightly kicked one boot against the doorframe, nodded again, and left. She knew he meant well. He was three years older than she was and had always been protective of her. With Pa gone, she was all the family he had left, and he was the same for her. But starting tomorrow, he'd have Mary, and the two of them would build a family of their own. Laurie needed the freedom to find her own way.

She looked again at the Bible on the bookshelf, then thoughtfully took it down. Laying it on the desk, she opened it to the first pages, where the list of births, deaths, and marriages were neatly written in various hands by generations of Kerstetters. She traced her father's name, Arnold Kerstetter, and below it, the dates of his birth, his marriage to Emily Mansfield, and his death on March 14, 1880. She turned to the next page, to where Harvey's name was written above her own. As much as she treasured this reminder of her family, she'd leave it here for Harvey. He had a marriage to record tomorrow, after all.

On a whim, Laurie took out a pen and opened *Tom Sawyer* to the front pages. She carefully copied all the names and dates in as small and neat a script as she could manage. Just because she wasn't taking the Bible didn't mean she had to leave her history behind. When the ink was dry, she closed the books, put the Bible back on the shelf, and carried the novels to her room, where she'd pack them with the rest of her things.

***

The next few days were a whirlwind of wedding preparations and festivities, packing, and heartfelt goodbyes. Mary cried when the Martins came for Laurie. Harvey loaded her two trunks into the farm wagon and pulled her in for a brief but tight hug.

"You'd better write," he said gruffly. "And if you ever need help, send for me and I'll come."

Laurie nodded, her own throat too choked with tears to speak. For a panicked moment, she wondered wildly why she

CHAPTER 1

was leaving her only family in the world. But then Mr. Martin lifted her up onto the wagon seat, and she settled beside his wife, and she remembered that not all family was blood. The Martins had been their neighbors time out of mind, and their daughters were what she'd always imagined sisters to be. She turned to wave to the newlyweds as the wagon rolled away from the house, taking a last look at the farmhouse and barn and the rustling fields of tall, green corn. She felt a strange disconnectedness. Without Pa, the Kerstetter farm no longer felt like home.

The two-hour drive to Harrisburg passed quickly. Laurie chatted with the Martins about farm work, gardening, and the wedding. Before she knew it, they were surrounded by buildings, and the rattle of the wagon was joined by the noises of other conveyances and of people and animals all going about their business. Laurie had only been to Pennsylvania's capital a handful of times, but Mr. Martin drove confidently to a pleasant neighborhood full of neat brick homes. He pulled to a stop in front of one that looked like all the others except that it had a simple sign by the front door that said "seamstress," with a needle and thread etched beneath.

Mr. Martin hitched the horses to the nearest post and helped the two ladies down. When they knocked at the front door, a girl Laurie's age opened it, carrying a sleeping baby. Her straight blonde hair tumbling from its ribbons would have made her look frazzled if it weren't so typical of her.

"Laurie!"

Laurie knew her best friend would have shrieked aloud if it weren't for little Levi resting heavy in her arms, his head on her shoulder. Instead, her exclamation came out as a hoarse whisper, her eyes wide with delight.

"Mama! Papa! Come in!"

Mrs. Martin carefully pulled her younger daughter into a hug before passing her to go find and hug Beth. Laurie hugged Essie too, as tightly as she dared with Levi between them.

"I can't believe you came! I know you said you would, but I didn't think Harvey would let you."

"Oh, he's fought me on it ever since I told him my plan, but he's never been able to stop me from doing what I wanted."

Essie chuckled softly. "True—only your Pa could ever change your mind." Her face fell, and she put a hand on Laurie's arm. "I'm so sorry, Laurie. I know you miss him."

Laurie nodded, the all-too-familiar tears choking her again. "So much. Thank you for coming to the funeral."

"We wouldn't have missed it. Your family is our family."

Their whispered conversation was interrupted by Mr. Martin bringing in the first of Laurie's trunks. The girls made their way past the front parlor, which had been fitted up to be Beth's dress shop, complete with a full-length mirror and a stool to stand on for fittings. The next room was a smaller private parlor. In the back of the house, they found Beth and Mrs. Martin in the kitchen, both elbow deep in flour. Laurie and Essie exchanged a look. Leave it to Mrs. Martin to jump right into the cooking.

"Laurie! Welcome," Beth said, using one arm to brush loose wisps of white blonde hair off her forehead and giving her guest a warm smile. "Have you come to stay awhile, then?"

"I have," Laurie said, crossing the room to give Beth a careful hug. "Thank you for letting me stay. How much do I owe you for rent?"

Beth waved a floury hand. "Just enough to help with food. The rest I'll take in labor. I'd be completely drowning without

CHAPTER 1

Essie, and it's all the two of us can do together to keep on top of things." She leaned her head so it rested against Laurie's for a moment, an older-sister gesture that warmed Laurie's heart. "I'm sorry about the circumstances, but I'm glad you're here."

Laurie knew that, after Harvey, Beth was the best able to understand her grief at losing Pa. A year ago, Beth had lost her husband, Robbie, to a carriage accident when Levi was barely two months old. That had been when Essie had moved from the farm to help her, watching the baby while Beth built her seamstress work from a hobby her husband supported into a business that would support her little family.

"I'm glad too," Laurie said, meaning it. "I can do whatever you need—cooking, cleaning, sewing…. Essie may only be good for rocking a baby and chatting with customers, but you know I can sit still long enough to sew a straight seam." Laurie grinned at Essie, who stood just inside the kitchen door, swaying slightly as Levi fussed in his sleep. Essie stuck her tongue out at her, and Laurie felt for a second like she'd stepped back in time to when none of the girls had a single care in the world.

Levi's fussing soon led to him waking, and Essie soothed him while Beth washed her hands so she could take him. Laurie washed her own hands and jumped into the cooking. Before long, the five of them were sitting down to eat, chatting merrily. After the dishes were washed and put away, Mr. and Mrs. Martin said their goodbyes and drove home, leaving Laurie to settle into her new life.

Chapter 2

Laurie soon discovered that her marriage prospects were no better in Harrisburg.

Not that there weren't plenty of gentlemen in the city. But Laurie's time was primarily spent helping Beth. Within the first two days, she realized that the sisters had each settled into their own role. Beth divided her time between Levi, sewing, and dress fittings. Before his death, Robbie had bought her a Singer sewing machine, an extravagant gift for his new bride. The time saved over needle and thread was the only thing that made her business possible, she told Laurie when she gave her a tour of the house the first day. There were three bedrooms upstairs: one that Beth shared with Levi, the guest room Essie had vacated to make space for Laurie, and Beth's sewing room, where a bed had been put along the wall opposite Beth's sewing table for Essie.

"You can't give up your room for me!" Laurie had protested when she learned of the sleeping arrangements.

Essie waved her off. "I've been sharing a room with Beth all my life. You're used to a room to yourself. I'm just so glad you're here!" And she enveloped Laurie in such a tight hug that all further arguments died.

Essie did a little of everything around the house, cooking,

cleaning, serving customers, and watching Levi. It was easy for Laurie to step in and pick up the slack. She took over most of the cooking and cleaning, since it was familiar work, and she was used to being up with the sun. Beth's sewing machine made quick work of the main seams of the garments, but most of the trim was still added by hand, and Laurie spent any down time with a needle and thread. She also changed her fair share of Levi's diapers.

So, despite the fact that there must be gentlemen of a suitable age and disposition somewhere in Harrisburg, Laurie rarely met them. She spent more time with the ladies who came into the shop, and occasionally with the young mothers and nannies with their children in the park when she accompanied Essie and Levi on a walk. There were a wider variety of people at church on Sunday mornings, but Laurie wasn't brazen enough to introduce herself to strangers, and Beth was too preoccupied with trying to get Levi to sit without fussing to socialize.

By the end of her second week staying with her friends, however, Laurie had decided she didn't much want to marry a Harrisburg gentleman anyway. She hated the city. Not that Harrisburg was a bad city; it was simply a city. She missed the country—the wide, sweeping farmland, the creeks that cut through the fields, and the broad shade trees. Harrisburg was crowded, dirty, and hot. So hot. Summer would be sweltering anywhere, but the crush of buildings didn't allow for a single cooling breeze. And the heat only made the city smells—including sweaty, often unwashed people and horse dung—that much worse.

During one walk to the park, Essie confided to Laurie that she hated the city too. "I've tried to convince Beth to move back to the farm with Mama and Papa. It was only Robbie and his job with the bank that kept her here in the first place. But she'd have to give up her new business, and she likes sewing for customers." Essie sighed. "She needs my help too much for me to go home without her."

Laurie felt for Essie's predicament. Her own situation was uncomfortable enough. She refused to go back to the farm, but she felt like she was relying too much on her friends' generosity. She was in an awkward kind of limbo, an in-between place where her life was on hold. She couldn't go back, but she didn't yet know how to go forward. What she wanted more than anything, what she'd been hoping to find here, was a home, a place to belong again. But Harrisburg would never be that for her. It was time to make a new plan.

She was still struggling to come up with one a week later when Essie called her into the front parlor. The last customers had just left. Laurie had been dusting in the hall while she waited for dinner to finish in the oven. Beth had taken the dress from the last fitting back to the sewing room; Levi was napping in his crib in the bedroom.

Essie waved her over to a chair by the front window where the westering sun shone brightly. A sheet of newsprint lay unfolded on her lap.

"Come look at this." Essie grinned. "I overheard the customers talking, and when they left this behind, I couldn't help myself. They're advertisements for mail-order brides."

"What?" Laurie dropped her duster on a chair by the door and crossed to sit beside her friend. "What do you mean?"

"Haven't you heard of them? Apparently, there are so few women out West that men have taken to placing ads in newspapers back East, looking for brides. They're great fun to read." She turned her attention back to the paper. "Look—this

CHAPTER 2

one has a sheep farm. And this one is a widower with three children looking for a woman who knows how to cook."

"Why would anyone answer an ad like that?" Laurie asked, peering over Essie's shoulder. "The West is perfectly lawless, isn't it? There are saloons and gunfights and whatnot."

"Oh, but think of the fun!" Essie said dreamily. "Men have had the adventure all to themselves for decades, and now we finally have a chance to join in."

"We?"

Essie waved her hand vaguely. "Ladies in general. Not me, obviously—I can't leave Beth. *You* could, though. Think of the wide open country. A homestead miles away from a city. Isn't that exactly what you want?"

Laurie pressed her lips together to hide a smile at her friend's exuberance. Essie's thirst for excitement was legendary. "The homestead, maybe, but not a marriage to a man I've never met."

"Oh, but you'd write to each other and fall in love through letters." The dreamy tone was back. "Read these with me. You probably won't find any you like, anyway—most of them are awful, just looking for a woman to keep house, not even the slightest bit romantic. But they're still fun to read."

They spent the next half hour reading through the ads, laughing at most of them and imagining what the writers might be like. One ad caught Laurie's eye, though she wasn't sure why: *Young rancher looking for a good cook in Haven River Falls, Wyoming.* It was on the short end, as far as the ads went, and really didn't say much about the man who wrote it. Laurie laughed over it with Essie before moving to the next one. But as she pulled dinner out of the oven later, the paper folded and put away, she couldn't get the name of the town out of her head. Haven River Falls. It had a nice ring to it. Laurie had loved playing on the banks of the Susquehanna River growing up. And a haven was a safe place to rest, wasn't it? That was exactly the kind of place Laurie was looking for.

But was she really crazy enough to answer an ad for a mail-order bride? Harvey would be appalled that she was even thinking about the idea. And she wasn't *really* contemplating it, was she? It was just a silly notion Essie had planted in her head. That was the problem with being friends with Essie—her wild ideas would get you into trouble if you followed them.

Over the next few days, though, the name Haven River Falls teased at the corners of her mind. When she was alone one morning, after breakfast but before the first customers were likely to arrive, Laurie dug out the paper and looked again at the ad. Still so little information. His name was Todd Knowles, he had a ranch, and he was apparently not the best cook. It said he was a *young rancher*, so she could assume he wasn't twice her age, though there was some leeway in the term. And he lived in Haven River Falls.

She put the paper away again, but a question nagged at her: was there any harm in writing a letter? She needn't agree to anything, and she certainly wouldn't be boarding a train anytime soon. But she could ask him for more information. Surely there was no harm in that?

Another two days passed while she wrestled with the question, but finally she gave in. One letter couldn't hurt, and at least she'd have answers. She waited until Sunday afternoon when there were no fittings. Beth and Essie took Levi on a stroll to the park, but Laurie stayed home, ostensibly to rest. When they were gone, she took out a sheet of paper and a fountain pen and sat down to write.

CHAPTER 2

To Mr. Knowles,

I read your advertisement in the paper, and I am curious to know more. I am nineteen years old. I am a reasonably good cook—nothing to write accolades about, but I've received no complaints from my father or cousin. I am also well versed in running a household, as I've managed my father's home for the past six years. Unfortunately, my father passed away a few months ago, and I find myself uncertain as to my future.

If I meet with your approval so far, please write me with more detail about you, your ranch, and your town. I am not prepared to commit to anything at this time, but perhaps that will change as I learn more about you.

Best wishes,
Laurie Kerstetter

Reading it over, Laurie made a face. She'd written dozens of better letters in her life. It was so stilted and formal. But what could one expect when writing to a complete stranger? She hated that she'd sought his approval when she didn't know whether *she'd* approve of *him*, but getting to know someone was a two-way street. He may not want to continue the acquaintance. If he didn't, she was at no loss.

She shrugged to herself, folded the letter into an envelope, and addressed it. It would go out in the mail on Monday.

Chapter 3

Laurie didn't tell Essie about sending the letter until an envelope arrived for her nearly two weeks later. Essie had gotten the mail, and she brought the letter into the kitchen, waving the envelope in front of Laurie, who was preparing lunch.

"Who's this letter from?" Essie turned the envelope so that she could read the return address. "Haven River Falls, Wyoming. Why does that sound familiar?"

Laurie blushed bright red, which couldn't fail to catch her friend's eye.

"You didn't!" Essie exclaimed. "You answered one of the ads?"

"I just wrote to ask for more information," she defended. "Haven River Falls is such a nice name for a town, and the advertisement was so vague."

"I thought you couldn't imagine why anyone would answer an ad for a bride?" Essie teased.

"I still can't," Laurie admitted. "It was a fool idea that *you* planted in my head. And yet, I couldn't rest until I knew more."

"Well, given how thick this envelope is, I'm sure this letter has all the information you need." Essie grinned. "Will you let me read it?"

CHAPTER 3

"We'll see." Laurie would probably let her; she'd end up telling her everything anyway. But she wanted to read it herself first.

The rest of the day was too busy to read. It wasn't until Laurie had retired to her room that night that she could sit at her small dressing table and unfold the letter by candlelight.

My dear Miss Kerstetter,

Thank you for your letter. I am terribly sorry for your father's loss and wish you all the best as you plan your future. I admit that I hope you decide I have a place in it.

I am not sure what to tell you about myself, so I will just say that I am not yet thirty; I am tall, with dark hair and blue eyes; and I am in good physical condition. Most of my time is spent working the cattle and doing the other tasks required on a ranch.

We finished with the spring cattle drive a couple months ago, moving the herds to their summer pasture. We'll soon be driving some of the older cattle to market, and in the fall we'll separate the spring calves from their mamas and brand them. Then they will all be driven to their winter pastures. The rest of the year is spent growing and storing hay, checking the cattle for illnesses, and doing a host of other things.

I've been living in Haven River Falls for going on four years now. It's a big name for such a tiny town. There's a mercantile, a small church, a saloon, and a boarding house. The owner of the boarding house also serves as the town barber. Most folks around either have nearby homesteads or work on a handful of small ranches, though there are those who work in the coal mines as well. As you might expect, ladies here are in short supply.

Haven River Falls is a six-hour ride south of Table Rock, a stop along the Union Pacific Railroad. It's wild country, with wide grassy plains between mountain ridges, though there are some odd land formations, like what Table Rock is named after. Story has it that the Haven River was named by the first settlers to come through here, who were so tired and thirsty that the river seemed like a gift from heaven. It is beautiful, and sometimes during a dry summer, the only green you'll see is on its banks.

I hope that's enough description to hook your interest. I'd be pleased to receive a description of you, if you'd be so good as to write again.

Yours,
Todd Knowles

Laurie read the letter twice through. She didn't know what to make of Mr. Knowles. His description of himself was nearly as bare bones as the ad in the paper. Clearly, the man didn't like talking about himself. When writing about the town and countryside, on the other hand, he bordered on poetic. And his penmanship—it wasn't as neat as Beth's, for instance, but it was lighter and more delicate than she would have imagined for a big man who worked with his hands. Laurie tried to form some kind of mental picture of the man who'd written the letter, but she soon had to give up.

She folded the letter, blew out her candle, and climbed into bed, her mind still pondering the letter. While she couldn't decide what she thought of Mr. Knowles, her imagination was caught by Haven River Falls and the plains and peaks around it. She'd lived all her life surrounded by the rolling hills of Pennsylvania, where the valleys they hemmed in were green and lush and perfect for farming. It was beautiful, and she loved it, but she felt a hint of excitement at the prospect of seeing something new. To get a glimpse of wilder country.

By the time she woke the next morning, she'd decided to

CHAPTER 3

write back to Mr. Knowles and hopefully draw out more detail about him—his likes and dislikes, anything to suggest what his personality might be.

Dear Mr. Knowles,

Your description of Haven River Falls makes me more curious than ever to see it. I've lived all my life in Pennsylvania, so I'm used to hills and valleys, but certainly nothing like the rugged terrain I've heard of out West.

In response to your request, I'm a bit short, only a few inches above five feet, and my hair and eyes are both light brown. I have a tendency to freckle when I'm out in the sun without a bonnet, which happens more often than my mother would have approved of. I just love the feel of the wind in my hair, and it's worth living with the freckles.

I'm currently staying with two of my dear friends, Beth and Essie, who are like sisters to me. I have no actual siblings, just my friends and my cousin who was raised with me. Do you have family? Do they live near you? Beth is a widow with a baby boy, so Essie and I help her with him and with keeping house while she works as a seamstress. She has always been the best dressmaker I know, and I've been learning a lot from her.

I know that ranching takes most of your time, but is there something that you enjoy doing with any free hours? I enjoy reading, when I have a minute, and though normally I knit and sew by necessity, I do enjoy those tasks. I've also found that I enjoy playing with Beth's son, Levi. He is old enough to crawl and to stack blocks (and knock them over), so we have great fun when it's my turn to watch him.

What is your favorite food? I'm partial to apple pie.

Do you have a favorite pet—a dog or horse, perhaps, that is more than simply a working animal? I used to have goats, which I loved, and my cousin had a mutt that followed him everywhere. And I always made friends with the barn kittens whenever I could.

I look forward to hearing from you again soon.
Sincerely,
Laurie Kerstetter

Laurie addressed the letter and put it out in the mail before she could second guess herself. This letter felt more significant than the last. The first letter was just to gather information. This one... This one still sought details but leaned a bit more toward instigating a friendship, at the very least. Was she really considering building any kind of relationship with this man?

Laurie wished for the thousandth time that her mother were still alive to advise her. Pa would probably be as horrified as Harvey to hear that she was corresponding with a stranger. But if Pa were alive to disapprove, then the farm would still be her home, and she wouldn't be in a position to consider a mail-order bride ad in the first place. She knew the men of her family would want to protect her above all, but maybe this time protection wasn't what she needed.

Without Mama to talk to, Laurie decided to confess the secret to Beth. Beth had been married, after all, and she had four years more wisdom to offer. When they'd sat down to dinner, Laurie cleared her throat.

"Beth, I have... well, I have a situation to ask you about."

Essie had just taken a big bite of pork chop, so she couldn't jump in with questions about the letter, but her wide eyes and fidgeting showed how hard it was for her to hold them in.

"What about?" Beth frowned.

"I've... I've responded to one of the ads in the paper—you

know, the ones from men out West looking for brides?"

"You've what?" Beth's fork clattered onto her plate, and beside her in his high chair, Levi froze, his eyes wider even than Essie's.

"I just asked for more information," Laurie hurried to assure her. "The ad was so short, and I liked the name of the town, and…" She trailed off at Beth's incredulous stare.

"*Why*, though?" Beth asked. "You have a home here with us for as long as you want it—and don't feel like you're imposing. I know you, Laurie Kerstetter. You've been such a huge help with the housework and with the sewing; it's been wonderful to have you with us. I should have told you sooner and more often."

"It's not just that…" It was partly that, though. Beth was right. For all that these sisters felt like her own family, she still felt like a temporary, if welcome, guest in Beth's home.

"You know I'll never speak against you getting married if you find someone you really like, but why consider marrying a stranger across the country? Aren't there men enough in Harrisburg? If you give it a bit more time, someone local could catch your eye."

"I haven't met any yet, and I'm not sure I want to. I don't want to stay in Harrisburg forever. I'm not a city girl."

Beth's expression softened. "No, you're not," she agreed. "And this gentleman—what does he do?"

Before Laurie could tell her about Mr. Knowles and his ranch in Wyoming, a knock sounded on the back door. Beth frowned and got up to answer it. In the weeks that Laurie had been staying here, only one person ever came to the kitchen door. Sure enough, Harry Ellis, Beth's brother-in-law, stepped into the kitchen.

"Forgive me for interrupting," he said, removing his hat and giving a small bow. "I was just on my way home from the office and thought I'd check in to see how you're doing. Do you need anything, Beth?"

"Nothing, thank you. We're doing quite well."

"You look well and happy. How is your little business doing?"

Beth raised a blonde eyebrow at his tone. Laurie bit the inside of her cheek to keep her own composure. He had no call to be looking down on Beth's work.

"It's growing every day," Beth said calmly. "I already have about as many orders as I can handle, and Laurie's proven a big help with the sewing."

"Good. Good." Mr. Ellis flicked the tiniest glance to Laurie before focusing back on Beth. "You'll let me know if there's anything I can help with, won't you?"

"Of course. Thank you for your concern."

Harry Ellis bowed and left. Laurie frowned after him. She couldn't pinpoint what she didn't like about him, aside from his condescending attitude, but she was glad he was gone.

"Why does he always stop at dinnertime?" Essie grumbled.

"He was on his way home from the bank." Beth resumed her seat.

"I think he was hoping you'd invite him to stay and eat with us," Essie said.

Beth pressed her lips together, and Laurie saw her nostrils flare. Beth didn't seem to like her brother-in-law much more than Laurie did.

"If Harrisburg gentlemen are like him, I'd rather look out West," Laurie muttered.

"You might be better off," Beth agreed, then bit her lip. "That was unfair of me. Robbie was..." She took a deep breath, and

CHAPTER 3

her voice sounded a little choked. "He was so caring and supportive. Nothing like his brother."

Laurie reached across the table to take Beth's hand, and Essie scooted out of her chair to stand behind her sister and wrap her shoulders in a hug.

After a moment, Beth let go of Laurie's hand and waved Essie away. "Enough of that. Tell me about this western fellow."

So Laurie told them both about Mr. Knowles, and at Essie's urging, she slipped up to her room to get the letter to read aloud to them.

"I like the idea of living on a ranch," Laurie admitted. "It's a bit different from a farm, but I expect a lot of the work is the same, and anything new, I can learn."

"I still don't like it," Beth said, leaning her chin on her hand. Their empty plates had been pushed to the side and forgotten for the moment. "You'd make a fantastic ranch wife—you have all the experience you need, except wrangling cattle, and I doubt he'd expect you to do that. But you know so little about him, and Wyoming is so far away."

"Well," Laurie said slowly, "if we keep writing each other, I'll get to know him better. I'm not planning to run off to Wyoming right this minute."

"Of course not," Essie agreed. "But it does sound like an adventure, doesn't it?"

Beth shot her a sharp look. "Don't you be getting any ideas. Ma and Pa would have my hide if I let you run off as a mail-order bride."

"Don't be ridiculous. You and Levi need me too much. Isn't that right, little one?" She made a silly face at the baby, who laughed and blew a raspberry.

Chuckling, the three women cleaned up the kitchen together

before moving to the sitting room. Essie played on the floor with Levi while Beth and Laurie tried to get some more sewing in before it was too dark to see.

Chapter 4

Mr. Knowles's next letter was somewhat more informative but altogether too short, considering that she'd waited a month for it to arrive.

My dear Miss Kerstetter,

I admit to liking the wind in my hair too, though a good cowboy wouldn't be caught without his trusty Stetson. The brim's shade is essential, since around here, trees are sparse.

I do like apple pie, but I'm partial to steak and potatoes.

I've got no family. I had a sister, but she and my parents died when I was fifteen. I hired onto my first cattle drive then, and I've been riding the range ever since. My horse, Buck, has been with me for most of that time, and I guess he's as much a friend as any I've had, but he's not a pet.

Like you say, I don't have much free time, except during winter, but I do like playing a game of cards now and then.

Yours,
Todd Knowles

Laurie felt for the poor, orphaned boy Mr. Knowles had been, taking on a man's work at a young age in order to support himself. Her own recent loss only amplified her sympathy.

They were both orphaned, both needing to find their own way. She was still reluctant to commit to this man for a lifetime, but her resistance was weakening.

"I'll never get to know him by letter," she complained to Essie after showing her friend the latest. "He's not very forthcoming. We could be writing for years before I have any idea what he's actually like."

"You could go west and meet him in person," Essie offered. "He said there's a boarding house in town, right? You could stay there while he courts you."

"Don't mail-order brides usually get married right away as soon as they arrive?" She had been listening more closely to the gossip during fittings, particularly when she heard this topic arise.

Essie shrugged. "Some even get married by proxy beforehand. But that doesn't mean you have to."

Laurie frowned. Once again, a madcap idea of Essie's had lodged in her head. It was lunacy to travel out to Wyoming to meet a man she'd only exchanged four letters with. It was exactly the kind of ridiculous behavior that made her question the sanity of any woman choosing to become a mail-order bride, although she could acknowledge that there were probably life circumstances that might make it a woman's only choice. But she wasn't in such dire circumstances. She had a place to stay, friends who loved her.

But not a home. Not somewhere that was *hers*.

She spent days arguing all angles with herself, sometimes in favor of Essie's suggestion but mostly against. To hop on a train on a whim and cross the country to a lawless place where she knew no one…. Harvey would haul her back to the farm and lock her up if he knew what she was thinking. She was sure

CHAPTER 4

Beth wouldn't like the idea either. Essie's approval couldn't be allowed to count for much.

But the more she thought about it, the more reasonable the idea appeared. If she was serious about pursuing a potential relationship with Mr. Knowles, letter writing was not the way to do it. Mail out West was simply too sporadic, and he was not the most effusive correspondent. Getting to know each other in person was the only viable choice. And if that was the case, winter was the ideal time. The rhythms of ranch life meant that once spring arrived, Mr. Knowles would likely be out working the cattle from sun up to sun down, and Laurie wouldn't get more than a few minutes a day in his company. If she traveled west soon, she'd likely arrive just after the autumn cattle drive and have his full attention.

A wistful, nostalgic corner of Laurie's mind thought that if they got along particularly well, they could marry within a few weeks, and she'd have a home in time for Christmas.

Essie's idea had so distracted Laurie that she hadn't responded to Mr. Knowles's letter. Now she wondered what to say. Should she send another likes-and-dislikes letter? Or should she tell him what train to expect her on?

At this point, she'd spun her mind in so many circles that her only choice for clarity was to lay it all out for her friends. So after dinner, while she stitched velvet trim onto a burgundy wool dress, Laurie told Beth about Essie's idea and listed the pros and cons of the plan.

Beth shot Essie a scowl. "Why would you even suggest such a thing? Single and alone in a town of men? Thousands of miles from friends and family?" She turned her glare on Laurie. "And you know better than to listen to anything my sister tells you. Hasn't she gotten you into enough scrapes?"

"She has," Laurie admitted with an apologetic smile at Essie. "But that doesn't mean I love her any less, and it doesn't mean that this idea is an awful one. It's bold, I'll give you that, but there's some logic to it, too."

"Can't you exchange letters for a few more months before you jump into this?"

"Laurie hates the city, Beth," Essie said. "I've seen it weighing on her for weeks."

"But it's not so hot now that October has come," Beth pointed out. "And you can see the leaves starting to change colors at the park."

Laurie sighed. "But seeing nature in a park is not the same as living in it. The buildings stifle me, and there are too many people. I don't know if I could bear it if I didn't have a garden to plant in the spring."

Beth sighed. "You're old enough to decide for yourself. I won't stop you if you insist on leaving, but I am still very firmly against it."

Laurie wasn't surprised by Beth's position, but she was surprised by her own reaction to it. Rather than influencing her toward safety and caution, Beth's disapproval solidified Laurie's resolve to go. Staying longer with her friends would only delay her future, not change it. Now that she'd heard of Haven River Falls and opened her mind to a new life out West, nothing less would be enough.

The next day, Laurie set about arranging the details of her trip. She used half of the money she'd gotten for the goats to purchase a train ticket to leave in two weeks. She drafted a short letter to Mr. Knowles, informing him of her travel details and requesting that he bespeak a room for her at the boarding house. Hopefully, if she sent it now, it would arrive well before she did.

Then she began to plan.

She didn't want to travel with her trunks, especially as she'd never traveled by train before. It would be easier, she thought, if she limited herself to one carpetbag that she could carry on her own. Unfortunately, deciding that meant that she needed to decide what to leave behind. Essie had promised to send the trunks along later, whenever Laurie wrote to ask for them. In the end, Laurie packed one nice dress for Sundays and two ordinary dresses. Nightclothes and undergarments were a must, plus a sweater and her warm wool coat, hat, and scarf for winter. She didn't have much space left, but she squeezed in her two precious books, Mama's wedding ring, and some practical things, like a set of knitting needles and her tiny sewing kit. As a going away present, Beth gave her a pair of lined leather gloves. Essie gave her a small stationery set, with a new fountain pen and a dozen sheets of paper.

"I don't know how well stocked their mercantile is," she said, "but now you have no excuse not to write to us."

"Have you written to Harvey yet to tell him?" Beth asked.

Laurie bit her lip and shook her head. Perhaps it wasn't fair of her to keep this from her cousin, but she didn't think he'd be as restrained in expressing his disagreement as Beth. "I'll mail his letter the day before I leave."

Beth pursed her lips but said nothing.

Chapter 5

The day of her departure came. Beth, Essie, and Levi all came to the station to see her off. Her friends sniffed and brushed away tears as they hugged her, and even baby Levi looked solemn and uncertain, but Laurie couldn't help the swell of excitement that buoyed her. Whatever happened with Mr. Knowles, she was on an adventure to new places, and she'd get to see for herself if Haven River Falls lived up to its name.

Her excitement had waned significantly by the end of her second day aboard the train. It was more comfortable than a wagon, she'd give it that, and she enjoyed watching the scenery rushing by. But she had chosen a cheaper ticket that didn't include a private sleeping compartment, so she had to make do with napping in her seat. The motion of the train was too bumpy to make this comfortable, and whenever she did sleep, she woke with a stiff neck and a growing headache.

The car wasn't packed, but it was full, and she spent most of her time sitting across from Mrs. Redmond, a middle-aged woman with soft features and a long neck. She was going to Nevada, she said, to stay with her son. His wife was expecting her first child, and as she had no family, Mrs. Redmond was determined to step in and help them adjust to life with a little one.

"And where are you off to, dear?" she'd asked early on the first day.

"Haven River Falls, Wyoming," Laurie said. "I'm... I've been exchanging letters with a gentleman there, and I'm going to meet him in person, see what he's like."

Mrs. Redmond's eyes widened. "You're one of those mail-order brides? Well, I'll be. I never would have guessed you for one."

"I haven't agreed to marry him," Laurie said, "and he hasn't actually asked me yet. But I suppose, strictly speaking, I am."

The entire train journey took four days. Laurie took every opportunity to get off when the train stopped to walk around. Most of the stations, especially as they got farther west, were merely a small building and a platform with nothing but prairie in all directions.

Table Rock, she was disappointed to discover, was one of these. She disembarked, clutching her carpetbag tightly. There was a bit of a bustle as the railroad workers refilled the train's water tank and unloaded a stack of crates and barrels by the stationmaster's office. Then the locomotive rumbled along the rails and puffed away, leaving Laurie standing alone on the platform. Her heart pounded as she surveyed the wide, flat, lonely plain. She'd told Mr. Knowles when her train was expected to arrive. Had he not received her letter?

In the distance to the north, she could see a smallish cabin and outbuildings, and a figure approached from that direction. When he stepped onto the platform, she could see he was about her father's age, his mussed, graying hair and droopy mustache making him look like an old, sleepy hound. His steps faltered when he noticed her. He gaped. "Did you miss getting back on the train before it left?"

"No, sir," Laurie quickly assured him. "I'm supposed to be here. I'm trying to get to Haven River Falls. It's south of here, isn't it?"

"Sure it is." The man smoothed a hand over his mustache and nodded. "But it's a long way if you ain't got a horse. Someone know you're coming?"

"I sent a letter." Laurie shrugged, her nervous heart still unpleasantly fluttery.

"Well, why don't you come in and have a drink—I keep a pitcher of water on the table just inside—and we'll figure out how to get you there."

The inside of the stationmaster's office was just one small, square room, with crates and barrels and all manner of things piled along one wall, and a table with a single chair against another. "'Scuse the mess. I store anything coming for the folks of Haven River Falls or roundabouts in here until they can come for it. My wife and I live just yonder. I walk over whenever a train comes to make sure everything's squared away." He waved toward the little homestead she'd seen north of the tracks.

"How often do trains come through?" Laurie asked, accepting a cup of water and sipping it.

"Every couple days, going one direction or the other."

A sound behind her made Laurie pause with the cup halfway to her lips again, and the stationmaster moved into the doorway to see past her. His face brightened.

"Good news, miss. That there's Wes Harrison from the mercantile out in Haven River Falls. Once he's got his wagon loaded, I'll bet there'll be room for a little thing like you."

He strode past her to greet the newcomer. The man's wide-brimmed hat made it impossible to see his face from this distance. He set the brake and saw to the horses, then the two men loaded the stack of crates from the train into the back of the wagon.

"You got room for a passenger?" She overheard the stationmaster ask.

The man tipped his hat back on his head as he looked up at her. He smiled amiably at her and nodded. "Course. You headed for Haven River Falls, miss?" He raised his voice so that she could hear him easily.

"Yes, please," Laurie said, crossing the platform toward him.

"Let me finish loading up, and we'll get you settled." The men made a few more trips back and forth to the office for more crates, then he helped her onto the seat and set her carpetbag amid the goods in back. He climbed up onto the bench beside her, then, with a wave to the stationmaster, he got the horses moving, drawing the wagon onto an unmarked, packed dirt track.

"Thank you," Laurie called to the older man. "And thank you," she added more quietly, casting a glance at the driver. From here she could see that he was not too old, probably in his early thirties, with a round face and clear, gray eyes. She liked the easy smile he gave her.

"Glad to help," he said. "You're lucky you came when you did—this is my last run to restock the store before winter. There won't likely be anyone else out this way for months."

Laurie's stomach clenched. She hadn't considered such a possibility.

"You visiting someone?"

"Sort of. I've been exchanging letters with a gentleman here—a Mr. Todd Knowles. I was hoping to meet him and see if we're compatible."

He nodded slowly. "I see." His glance was curious, but he didn't pester her about being a mail-order anything. "I don't know him, but there are a lot of folks working on the ranches roundabout, and I can't say I've met them all."

"I'm sure you do meet a lot of people, though, running a mercantile."

He nodded with another smile. "I do, and I enjoy it."

Though Mr. Harrison was easy to talk to, Laurie was soon distracted. Seeing the countryside out the window of a fast-moving train was not the same as driving through it in a wagon. The wide prairie wasn't at all what Laurie had pictured when she'd thought of Wyoming. The Rocky Mountains should be here somewhere, and with a name and reputation like theirs, she'd thought they'd be obvious despite the cloudy, gray sky.

She caught Mr. Harrison watching her staring at the dun-colored grassland. "It's not what I pictured," she explained sheepishly. "Where are the mountains?"

He pointed ahead. "The low clouds hide them. You'll see them soon enough. I hope you're prepared for a long ride."

Laurie was, but she was surprised by how fast the hours passed. Mr. Harrison asked her about where she'd come from and her journey on the train, and when they weren't talking, she was gazing at the land around them. It was nothing at all like the rolling, green, forested hills of Pennsylvania. Everything was flat, and the tall grasses rustled in the breeze. Laurie decided that she liked the sound—it reminded her of how her mother used to shush her gently to sleep as a child.

True to Mr. Harrison's prediction, when they stopped to rest the horses after another hour or two, Laurie was able to see the mountains through the low cloud cover. Or at least their lower

CHAPTER 5

reaches. They stretched stark and gray into the obscuring mist so that Laurie couldn't begin to guess at how tall they were. They cut across the land, filling Laurie's vision east to west.

"Do we have to go over the mountains?" She gasped as the idea popped into her head.

"Not over—through," Mr. Harrison said. "You can't see it today, but there's two peaks. The Haven River flows down from the one on the left. We'll be driving through the pass between them."

More time passed, and the ground beneath them rose, more and more sharply. Then, unexpectedly, to the right of the trail, another track turned off, marked by a wooden sign that merely had a large N with a circle around it.

"That's Newcomb Ranch," Mr. Harrison told her. "Most of the land we've been driving through is part of their spread. We're about halfway to town."

Laurie looked around even more curiously. Ranch land didn't look a bit different from prairie land, and there wasn't a single cow in sight. But perhaps the cattle were in a different pasture.

The trail climbed even more steeply and began to bend and twist in switchbacks. Laurie clung to the edge of the seat and tried not to give off any sign of nerves. Mr. Harrison grinned over at her once or twice, but he didn't comment. After what seemed like forever, the trail leveled out and then began to descend, and Laurie decided that she liked going downhill even less than she'd liked going up. She was afraid that all the weight in the wagon would carry them too quickly and overwhelm the horses, but Mr. Harrison knew how to handle his team, and he kept his hand on the brake to control their speed.

"Look," he said as they came around another switchback.

Laurie raised her eyes from the horses' backs and gasped. The whole countryside spread out in front of her. She thought she saw more mountains in the distance, just the feet beneath the clouds. Nearer were wide stretches of prairie like she'd been seeing for miles. But nearer still was a small cluster of buildings. It was all shades of brown and gray, between the dirt streets, the weathered wood, the clouds, and the dust, but there was something charming about it just the same. And off to the left, an oasis: trees and green grass seemed to cascade down the mountain and spill into the valley, hiding the river and falls from view but making it abundantly clear where to look for them.

Laurie's heart thrilled at seeing this place that she'd been imagining for so long. It was nothing like she'd expected, and yet it was everything she'd hoped for. As they descended the final miles and rumbled into town, her eyes jumped from building to building, impressed by the solid simplicity of their construction.

Mr. Harrison pulled the wagon to a stop in front of a two-story house with whitewashed clapboards. A wreath of dried flowers hung from the door.

"Here's the boarding house," he said, setting the brake. "I'll come in and see you settled with the Browns. And if you need anything, the mercantile is just there, at the end of the street."

Laurie thanked him, climbing down from the wagon as he jumped down and got her carpetbag. He carried it inside for her, setting it beside the door of the small parlor and removing his hat.

"A guest for you, ma'am." He nodded to the two ladies who rose from their chairs.

CHAPTER 5

The older woman was middle-aged and comfortable looking, with fading brown hair and a cheerful smile. The younger girl was obviously her daughter, with a matching smile and the same brown hair, but a lighter, more slender figure. She could only have been a few years younger than Laurie.

"A guest!" The mother gawked. "And a young lady!"

"Found her at the train station when I went for supplies," Mr. Harrison said. "Have you got a room available?"

"No, but we'll make space," the older woman said, tutting. "There's nowhere else to stay, not for a young lady."

"What's your name?"

"Laurie Kerstetter." She met the younger girl's direct gaze with a shy smile.

"Martha Brown," the girl introduced herself. "Mama, she can share my room. I can already tell we'll be great friends."

Mr. Harrison wished Laurie well and took his leave, promising to get a message to Mr. Knowles that she had arrived. As soon as the door closed behind him, Martha swept Laurie on a brief tour of the house. The parlor was at the front of the house on one side, the dining room on the other. The kitchen was behind the dining room, and the fourth quadrant of the downstairs was broken into two rooms for the family, one for Mr. and Mrs. Brown and one for Martha—and now Laurie.

"There are six bedrooms upstairs, all rented out, but you don't need to worry about the menfolk who live there—you'll only see them at meals, and they're, most of the time, polite," Martha said. "And if that's not enough, Deputy Cooper has one of the rooms, and he can be trusted to keep the others in line."

Laurie had to admit that she found the setup reassuring. Despite her bold talk to Beth and Essie before leaving, she'd been nervous to be a woman alone in a town full of men. But

Martha's apparent desire to adopt her into the family set her mind at ease, and she knew her friends back in Harrisburg would be relieved to hear it too.

They took her bag to the bedroom they'd be sharing, where Mrs. Brown was already rearranging the furniture so she could put up a cot for Laurie. "I apologize that it's not a proper bed, Miss Kerstetter," she said as she tucked sheets and laid out blankets and a pillow.

"It's perfect," Laurie said. "I can't thank you enough for your hospitality."

Mrs. Brown smiled. "It's our pleasure, dear. Dinner will be on the table momentarily." She bustled from the room.

Martha showed Laurie the pitcher and basin for washing so she could freshen up before they ate. "You can have a proper bath later, if you'd like, but I'm afraid there isn't time now."

"A bath would be divine," Laurie admitted. "I've worked on a farm all my life, yet somehow four days on a train make me feel dirtier than I've ever been."

She splashed her face and hands and fixed her hair, then the two made their way to the dining room while Martha chatted about the town. "Sorry for talking your ear off," she said after a few minutes, her cheeks turning pink. "There aren't any other girls my age around here."

"None?" Laurie asked. "Have you lived here all your life?" She couldn't imagine growing up without Beth and Essie at the farm next door.

"Every minute," Martha said. "Anna Mae Johnson is fourteen, but she lives on the ranch south of town, so I'm lucky if I see her once or twice a year. And Sarah Billings is twenty-one, but she got married and moved to Cheyenne two years ago. I guess there are a couple on the homesteads farther out, but

CHAPTER 5

they don't come to town much."

"Well, I don't mind your talking at all, and as you can see, my ears are both still attached." She grinned at the girl.

"Even so, it's my turn to listen. Tell me about the train."

So Laurie did, and she was describing Mrs. Redmond when three men joined them at the table. One was a stick-thin man about Mrs. Brown's age, with a handlebar mustache and the same sparkling hazel eyes as Martha's. She introduced her father, who bowed and welcomed Laurie pleasantly. He then introduced the other two men. One, a Mr. Jones, was a solid fellow who looked as though he'd come straight from the fields. His trousers and flannel shirt were dusty, and his hair was mussed from being covered in a hat all day. He looked startled to see an unfamiliar woman at the table, and he bashfully apologized for not cleaning up better before coming to dinner.

The other man was the Deputy Matthew Cooper that Martha had mentioned. He was tall and handsome, with strawberry blond hair and blue eyes. A dimple showed in his left cheek when he smiled in greeting. Laurie returned the smile, blinking in momentary surprise: Deputy Cooper's empty left sleeve had been knotted up and pinned out of the way. Amputees were not unheard of, particularly after the War Between the States, and even Mr. Martin was missing three toes from a farming accident. But the deputy couldn't have been old enough to have fought in the war; Laurie guessed him to be less than ten years older than herself. He would have been a child at the time. What kind of accident had caused the loss of his arm?

She'd never dream of asking, of course. Nosy curiosity like that would be the epitome of rudeness, and Mama had always insisted on good manners.

Their meeting was interrupted by Mrs. Brown and her cook

bringing out stew and biscuits and green beans. Mr. Brown said the blessing, and they all tucked in. Mr. Jones devoured his meal and quickly excused himself, clearly uncomfortable to be in the presence of an unfamiliar lady. Deputy Cooper spent some time discussing local affairs with the landlord, but he also joined the ladies' conversation at times, to ask Laurie where she'd come from and what had brought her to Haven River Falls. Laurie thought his brow furrowed briefly when she mentioned coming to meet Mr. Knowles, but it cleared quickly. Perhaps she'd imagined it, or maybe he was trying to think if he'd heard the name before.

At last, plates were empty, and Deputy Cooper pushed his back with a sigh. "Excellent dinner, as always, Mrs. Brown. I thank you." He smiled at Laurie. "You'll soon find that this wonderful family has a talent for making people feel at home. I've been boarding with them for two years, and it's like being part of a family again. Miss Brown even reminds me of my little sister."

Martha scrunched her nose and stuck out her tongue at him.

Deputy Cooper chuckled. "*Exactly* like my sister." He said goodnight and left the room.

When he was gone, Laurie glanced around the half empty table. "Didn't you say there were *six* occupied rooms upstairs?"

"Yes, but most aren't back in time for dinner every night. We'll keep everything warming on the stove for whenever they get in." Mrs. Brown rose and began to clear the table. Laurie and Martha got up to help.

When the meal was cleaned up, Laurie was able to get a much needed bath in the bathhouse out back. The water was lukewarm and cooling quickly, so Laurie scrubbed as fast as she could, but it felt beyond wonderful to have clean hair and skin again. Dressed and back inside, she submitted to Martha's pleading to let the girl comb her hair.

"Your hair is so pretty, and I never get to play with anyone's hair," Martha pouted. "We'll sit by the stove in the parlor so you can warm up."

Laurie had to admit that it was nice to sit by the fire and have Martha gently comb out all the tangles that had formed while she'd ridden the train. No one had dressed Laurie's hair for her since her mother had died. Between the gentle brush strokes and the warmth and dim firelight, Laurie felt dreamy and nostalgic, almost as if she and her new friend were in a world of their own.

Martha seemed to feel the same way because she said softly, "I wish there were more ladies in Haven River Falls." She paused her combing. "I wish there were a *lot* of things in Haven River Falls."

"Like what?"

"A school and enough children to fill it. A library and time to read all the books." Laurie could hear the wistful smile in her voice. "A sewing circle."

Laurie could only imagine what it would be like to grow up as one of the very few girls in such a tiny town. Though the area she'd grown up in was rural, she'd attended school, and there had been eight girls in her class. They hadn't had a public library, but the teacher had a bookshelf at the school that students could borrow books from.

"I've never been in a sewing circle either," Laurie said, choosing to discuss common ground. "Perhaps, once I'm settled, we can start one."

"It would only be you, me, and Mama," Martha pointed out. "Mrs. Harrison from the mercantile might join us, but she's often busy."

"Mr. Harrison's wife?" Laurie thought of the cheerful fellow who'd driven her from the train station.

"His mother," Martha said.

"Well, four ladies are better than none," Laurie pointed out. "We may have to settle for a sewing *square* for now."

Martha giggled and braided Laurie's hair, tying the ends with scraps of muslin.

Chapter 6

The next morning, Laurie breakfasted with the family and joined Martha in helping Mrs. Brown with the daily housekeeping. They dusted and swept the downstairs while the lady of the house saw to the boarders' rooms upstairs.

"It would go faster if we did the whole house together," Martha muttered to Laurie, "but I'm not allowed to set foot in the men's rooms, even when they're not here."

Laurie could understand Mrs. Brown's caution, but she agreed with her friend that it was inconvenient. When the chores were done, the three ladies decided to get some fresh air. They walked from one end of town to the other, which took very little time, with Martha pointing out all the buildings and telling her stories about the people who lived there. She had nothing to say about the saloon, though; a glance at her mother and a bright red blush were all that followed the information of what the building was.

"There are a few female residents," Mrs. Brown said primly, "but they don't leave the premises."

Laurie frowned. She'd heard of saloon girls who entertained the patrons by dancing with them and plying them with liquor, and who may also entertain in other ways. She shuddered.

What an awful life.

But it was the middle of the day, and the saloon was dark and quiet. They passed without incident.

As they were turning to walk back to the boarding house, Laurie commented on how few people they'd seen. She'd privately been hoping that she might run into Mr. Knowles while they were out.

"Most folks work on the surrounding ranches," Mrs. Brown said. "Those that don't are either working indoors today or are sleeping off last night." She shot a significant glance at the empty saloon.

Laurie was relieved to remember that the man she'd come to meet was a rancher, so he was unlikely to be in town this morning. "How might I go about finding Mr. Knowles? Mr. Harrison promised to pass on a message, but he wasn't familiar with Mr. Knowles. Who do you think might know him?"

"We'll ask Pete to take a message," Mrs. Brown said decisively. "That boy knows everyone and where to find them."

Martha leaned closer to Laurie. "He's ten, oldest of four children, and he runs errands for everyone."

She pointed to a young boy who was sitting on the mercantile steps in a patch of sunlight. He had red hair which Laurie thought would be even brighter if he weren't covered in so much dust and dirt. Mrs. Brown waved him over, and he jogged across the street to them, tipping his floppy wool hat as he skidded to a stop.

"What c'n I do for you, Miz Brown?"

Mrs. Brown looked to Laurie.

"Can you find Mr. Todd Knowles and tell him that Miss Kerstetter is staying at the boarding house and would like to meet him?"

CHAPTER 6

Pete nodded and accepted a penny from Mrs. Brown. "I'll send 'm over soon as 'e can."

"Thank you." Laurie gave the boy a smile, and he raced off.

Martha linked her arm through Laurie's. "Your fella will be here before you know it."

Her prediction wasn't quite accurate. Laurie was perfectly aware of time passing as they prepared and ate the noon meal and set to work on some mending. It was midafternoon when the front door opened and a tall figure in a Stetson and a canvas coat tromped in. Laurie and Martha set down their sewing as Mrs. Brown rushed in from the kitchen.

"Can I help you, sir?"

"Hope so," the man said, his voice carrying the roughness of years of smoking and drinking and hollering at cattle. "Name's Todd Knowles. Got a message Miss Kerstetter was stayin' here."

Mrs. Brown shot Laurie a look. Laurie slowly rose to her feet.

"I'm Laurie Kerstetter, Mr. Knowles." Her hands trembled, and her voice wavered a bit too. She wished she could see his face under that hat.

Her wish was granted as he lifted the hat from his head and nodded to her. "Mighty pleased to meet you, miss."

Laurie bit her lower lip hard. He was nothing like she'd pictured. He was tall, dark haired, and blue eyed, yes. But his wiry hair and whiskers stood out at all angles, and she couldn't guess at when he'd last had a trim or a shave. He turned away slightly to hang his coat and hat on the hooks by the door, revealing a shirt that probably used to be white and a pair of dusty wool trousers held up by suspenders. He looked wild and unkempt, and a whiff when he crossed the room told Laurie that it had been a while since he'd bathed as well.

"It's… It's a pleasure to meet you," she stammered, her mind racing. She'd come all the way from Pennsylvania to meet *this* man? Maybe he'd just come from working the ranch and hadn't had time to change from his work clothes, she reasoned hopefully. "Did you, um, get my letter that I was coming?"

"Sure did," he said. "Glad you made it alright. Reckon the preacher is around somewhere if you want to get hitched right away."

Martha reached over and clutched Laurie's hand. Laurie didn't need to look at her friend's face to know she was appalled at the idea.

"Not just yet, Mr. Knowles," she said politely. "I'm here to meet you and get to know you a bit before I decide about marriage."

Mr. Knowles looked disgruntled, but he nodded. "What do you want to know? I've got a place on the south end of town, not too big but cozy enough. You'll probably want to add fancy touches like curtains and whatnot, but you'll have to wait till I've signed on with another outfit in the spring. Got my pay to last through the winter, but not enough extra for frippery stuff."

Laurie frowned, confused.

Mr. Knowles went on, oblivious. "Hope you're as good a cook as you said, and the house could use some cleaning. I see you're handy at sewing too. That'll be good—got some mending that needs done."

The pit of Laurie's stomach sunk lower. The man truly only wanted a cook and housekeeper, not a genuine relationship. Except—

"And it'll be nice to have warm company on winter nights at my own home."

CHAPTER 6

Martha's hand tightened on Laurie's, and Laurie herself felt suddenly nauseated, first at the uncouth way he mentioned such a thing, and second at the hint that he was familiar with having "warm company" outside his home, presumably at the saloon.

Laurie gritted her teeth and steeled her spine to speak, choosing to ignore his most recent comments. "What did you mean by signing on to another outfit come spring?" she asked. "Remember, I'm new here and don't know ranching."

"I sign on with whatever ranch needs hands," Mr. Knowles replied, puffing up his chest as though he were proud to enlighten her ignorance. "They'll all be hiring for the spring cattle drive. I just finished up with the Opelski outfit a week ago."

"You're... a cowboy," Laurie said. "Your letters said you're a rancher." She looked at Martha and Mrs. Brown. "There's a difference, isn't there?"

Both of them nodded, but it was Mr. Knowles who answered. "Well, see, that's Stella's mistake. She's the one that wrote the letters—she was raised to be a proper lady before her family came west to escape the war, and she can read and write real good. I never learned, so she agreed to help me."

A cold feeling settled over Laurie. "Who's Stella?"

"One of the gals at the saloon. Sweet thing—you'll like her. I mighta stretched the truth when I first met her, an' she's still got it in her head that I own my own spread."

Laurie blinked at him, her whole body frozen except her eyes, which could only flutter in shock and horror. "So..." She could barely feel Martha's hand still holding hers. "So you're not a rancher, and you didn't write the letters. Your letters were written by a... a saloon girl named Stella?"

Mr. Knowles nodded. "She got most things right, though. My favorite meal is steak and potatoes, an' I did sign on with my first cattle drive after I lost my family."

Laurie remembered how she'd felt sympathy and a kind of connection when she'd read that fact in his letter. The letter that Stella the saloon girl wrote for him. She felt sick.

"Now that we know each other a bit, what say we head on over to the preacher?"

All she could do was numbly shake her head. Mrs. Brown came to her rescue. "One meeting isn't enough, Mr. Knowles. Miss Kerstetter needs more time. Perhaps you can call again tomorrow."

"Right." Mr. Knowles slapped his hands on his knees and pushed himself to standing. "I'm just eager to have you be mine, Miss Kerstetter. You're an even prettier thing than I was expecting."

Laurie wasn't sure what response she squeaked as the man strode to the door and put on his hat and coat. He tipped his hat in her direction before letting himself out.

Martha let go of Laurie's hand and put her arms around her shoulders. "That's not at all what I expected," the girl sighed.

Laurie covered her face with her hands. "Why did I come? I'm such a fool. Why didn't I listen to Beth?"

The front door opened again, and Laurie froze, peeking through a gap in her fingers, fearing a reappearance from the man who'd just left. Instead, it was Deputy Cooper, who frowned over his shoulder at someone outside before closing the door behind him and surveying the ladies in the parlor.

"Everything alright?" he asked. "Was that fellow bothering you ladies?"

"No," Mrs. Brown said, seemingly at a loss. "Not bothering."

CHAPTER 6

"That was Mr. Knowles," Martha said significantly, arching an eyebrow and giving Laurie's shoulders an extra squeeze.

"Ah." Deputy Cooper's frown deepened. "I'll leave you in privacy, then. But if you ever need anything, Miss Kerstetter, you just let me know."

"Thank you." Her hands muffled her words, but Deputy Cooper nodded and left.

"It was all lies," Laurie murmured, lowering her hands a little and leaning her head against Martha's. "I knew coming was a risk, but…" She shook her head. "He got my last letter. He knew I was coming, and he didn't come to meet me at the train. I would have been stuck there if Mr. Harrison hadn't come to pick up a shipment."

It was the least of the things wrong with Mr. Knowles and the situation, but it was the easiest to focus on. The lie about his job, his wish to marry her for the sake of essentially having a servant, his presumably intimate acquaintance with Stella… It was all more than she could think about right now.

"Maybe he improves on acquaintance," Mrs. Brown said with forced lightness. "There's no harm in meeting him again—we won't let you alone with him, of course—and you can give yourself time to decide." She got up from her chair and came over to sit on Laurie's other side. She rested a hand on Laurie's back and rubbed in gentle, motherly circles. "If you decide you'd rather not marry him, well, you're welcome to stay with us as long as you like. And there's no shortage of menfolk around here—I doubt it would take you long to find someone you like better."

"Thank you." Laurie pulled both mother and daughter into a hug. "I don't know what I would do without you."

"Run for the train station as fast as you could," Martha

muttered. "It's what I'd do. But I hope you'll stay."

Chapter 7

Mr. Knowles did not improve upon closer acquaintance. On the contrary, Laurie found more to dislike the more she saw of him. He called at the boarding house each day that week. He was rude and poorly behaved; he showed no signs of bathing. Sometimes he stank of spirits. Once he came ridiculously early, before the family had sat down to breakfast. Between the red rimming his eyes and the fog of perfume that hung around him, Laurie was certain that he'd spent the previous night at the saloon and hadn't yet gone home. Mr. Brown stepped in on that occasion to send the man home, declaring that no visitors were allowed at such an indecent hour.

Every day he asked if Laurie was ready to go see the preacher. And every time she put him off, he got more impatient and angry.

"I'm afraid I'll have to go back to Pennsylvania," Laurie said to Martha after Mr. Knowles left one afternoon. His face had gotten red as he demanded to know how long she'd make him wait. "I'm afraid of what he'll do if I turn him down outright, but I can't marry him."

"Can't you stay and marry someone else?" Martha pleaded.

"I wish I could."

Besides not wishing to return to Harrisburg or, worse, to Harvey and Mary at the farm, Laurie had fallen in love with the town of Haven River Falls. It wasn't much to look at, but it had so much potential. If some of Martha's wistful dreams for the town could come about, it would be a charming home. Laurie couldn't bring about an influx of ladies to civilize the place, but she was one lady, and she'd like to stay. She and Martha had spent one afternoon walking to the river and viewing the falls, which had filled Laurie with much needed peace. The grass on the river bank was still green, and there were low bushes that hadn't lost their leaves. The branches of the trees were bare, but Laurie could imagine coming for a picnic in the shade by the water in the summer.

Of course, the charm of her imaginary picnic was dimmed by the need for an escort—in the current case, Mr. Brown and his pistol. This was a shocking arrangement to Laurie, but Martha had seemed to expect it. Girls couldn't go anywhere alone, and no one went far in the West without a gun. Poor Martha had never known the freedom of running and playing alone in the fields and woods without fear.

Maybe if the town of Haven River Falls could be tamed, the next generation would know more freedom.

"Why can't you stay? Someone else will marry you, I'm sure."

"But I can't court anyone else without Mr. Knowles getting jealous and violent."

Martha frowned in thought. "Ask Deputy Cooper. He's a good man. I'd bet he'd marry you, and he's a lawman, so he could keep you safe."

Laurie shook her head. "I won't marry someone just for protection. I can't settle for anything less than the hope of love and a happy home."

CHAPTER 7

Martha made a face. "I don't see why you wouldn't have that with the deputy, but I do understand."

Laurie didn't know how to explain to her friend that while she liked Deputy Cooper, she didn't feel anything special for him. She didn't think he felt anything for her either—he treated her in a brotherly way, like he treated Martha.

Despite that conversation with Martha, Laurie was reluctant to leave. She couldn't help hoping to find another solution that wouldn't involve a long wagon ride to the train station so that she could return to her old friends like a chastised puppy with her tail between her legs. This whole disaster had been spurred by a series of Essie's ill-fated ideas, but Laurie had been the one to act on them, and she couldn't help but be embarrassed by the outcome.

Her hand was forced, however, when Mr. Knowles called on Monday morning. Laurie and Martha had been helping bake pies in the kitchen. Mrs. Brown was elbow deep in flour and butter and couldn't come out with them, but the girls met him in the parlor with all the doors open between the two rooms.

Mr. Knowles didn't bother taking the seat Laurie offered him. He stalked toward her. "Preacher today, Miss Kerstetter?"

"Not today," she said, her heart starting to race. The reek of spirits clung to him, and she hoped he wasn't too far under their influence.

"I'm losing my patience, girl," he growled. "I sent out an ad for you, and I'm gonna have you—married or not. I'll give you three days to make up your tarnal mind which it'll be."

Then he stalked out, slamming the door behind him. Laurie stood frozen, trembling.

Martha reached over and clutched Laurie's arm. "What are you going to do?"

Laurie took a deep breath. "Run for the train station," she said, repeating the words Martha had said after their first meeting with Mr. Knowles. "Thank goodness I only have the one bag. Will you help me?"

"Of course I will. I'll help you pack now. I'm sure once we tell Pa, he'll agree to drive you out tomorrow."

Laurie shook her head. She knew by now that a wagon leaving town would draw notice—the men at the livery would have to be involved, and no one had much business north of the mountains except Wes Harrison picking up supplies from the train station. And he'd said he wouldn't make any more trips this year. "We can't tell anyone. I can't risk Mr. Knowles finding out and coming after me. I know your parents would gladly help, but the more people who know, the harder it will be to keep the secret. I can sneak better on foot."

"On foot?" Martha gasped so loudly she clapped a hand over her mouth and glanced at the kitchen. Fortunately, the cook was humming something loud and off key, and no one heard her.

"Well, I can't steal a horse, and I can't buy one—I have *some* money Papa left me, but I've been paying room and board in one place or another for months."

"Laurie, this is a horrible idea," Martha protested.

"Worse than marrying Mr. Knowles?"

"No," the girl admitted. "Nothing's worse than that." Her hand gripping Laurie's arm tightened. "But it's not safe to be out alone."

"I expect the dangers to solitary women come from men like Mr. Knowles more than anything," Laurie said. "And there aren't many of those between here and Table Rock." She hoped to feign enough confidence to assure both Martha and herself,

CHAPTER 7

because she was just as worried as her friend. She'd feel a lot better if she had Papa's shotgun, even though her aim wasn't stellar. Of course, the gun had stayed on the farm with Harvey, and she couldn't afford to buy one of her own. But she'd rather take her chances with dangers in the wild than with the human predator here in town.

"Okay," Martha acceded grudgingly, "but promise me that you'll write to me at the very first stop—or even at Table Rock itself—letting me know that you got there safely."

"I will," Laurie said. "Now let's go help finish those pies before your mother comes looking for us. We can figure out the details later."

***

John Newcomb scrubbed a hand down his face, the stubble rough under his palm. He'd have to stop for a haircut and shave when he was in town tomorrow, since it would be his last for the winter. He sighed and looked over his scribbled list again, then cast his eyes over the contents of his cellar. This inventory was his least favorite task, but if there was one thing he'd learned in his seven years in Wyoming, it was the importance of being prepared. Jars and cans of produce lined shelves on the walls, and baskets on the floor nearly overflowed with potatoes, carrots, and turnips. Smoked ham and beef. Bacon. Smoked sausages. There was plenty of flour, but he'd want to pick up some more sugar and salt at the mercantile, and coffee too. They'd run out of salt and coffee less than halfway through their first winter out here, and George had been a bear in the morning without it.

The familiar twinge of loss at George's memory hit him, and

John frowned and climbed back up the ladder to the kitchen. This whole place was etched with memories of his brother, and two years hadn't faded them a jot.

He leaned against the sturdy wooden table, remembering more of that first year. They'd managed to store up enough hay to bring their meager herd through the winter, but they hadn't planned so well for themselves and had been left eating nothing but beans for the last two weeks before the snow melted from the pass and they could get into town for supplies. John made a face at the thought of those bland legumes—they'd had no salt or sugar or molasses or pork or anything to make them more palatable.

Only weeks later, George had arranged to pay Ivan Opelski—the oldest son of a nearby rancher—to come work with them for the summer and teach them what they needed to know so they could thrive in their new home, rather than surviving by the skin of their teeth. Opelski had called them both "city boy" at every opportunity, but they'd become friends by the end of the autumn roundup. It had been Ivan who had taught John how to can some of the garden's produce, so that subsequent winters at least included pickled beans and carrots and strawberry jam. The garden itself was only a success thanks to their sister, Missy. If it hadn't been for her love of plants, her penchant for growing things in pots on her balcony at their house in Boston, and her insistence that he help her with it, their garden plot would be a hopeless mess.

Those first couple years John had felt like a fish out of water. But he'd loved the wide-open spaces and impossibly fresh air too much to give up, and George's sense of adventure would never quit. They'd stuck with it, rebuilding the house, improving the barn, growing the herd. Now John could look

CHAPTER 7

out the small window at their—his—land with pride. The cattle had been rounded up and enclosed in the fenced winter pasture. Plenty of hay had been cut and stored in the barn's loft. The horses were healthy and freshly shoed. John had let go the seasonal hands he'd hired, promising them more work next year. Only Carlos remained, and John couldn't appreciate him enough. Not that a full-time cattle hand could ever replace his brother, but John needed the help to keep the place running, and he was glad not to be wholly alone through the winter months.

And according to John's inventory, they were nearly set. He just needed to make one final trip into town for a few more supplies before the first snow closed the pass.

***

The next morning saw Laurie creeping silently out the kitchen door in her stocking feet long before it was light. Martha held a lantern for her while she leaned against the wall to lace on her boots. Laurie hugged her friend before taking the lantern and picking up her carpetbag.

"Thank you," she whispered. "I'll write, I promise."

"You'd better," Martha hissed. "Be careful. I'll hold Mama off as long as I can."

With a last smile, Laurie hurried up the street toward the mountain. If she could just make it over the pass before the sun rose and revealed the lone traveler to everyone in the valley, she'd be set. She hoped.

It didn't take long to leave the buildings behind. Laurie tugged her hat low and pulled her scarf up so it covered half her face. It wasn't much of a disguise—there were so few women in town, anyone could guess who she was—but the deep gray wool helped her blend in with the dark, and it kept her face warm against the biting chill. The temperature had dropped overnight, far lower than she'd yet experienced it, and it looked to be a cold day.

"That's alright," she whispered to herself as she shivered and pulled her wool coat tighter. "The walk will warm me. And I'd rather be wearing my coat than carrying it." The carpetbag was heavy enough without it.

The track out of town was not as well worn as Laurie had expected, and she had some trouble following it. The ground began to climb. Sometimes Laurie followed the switchbacks; sometimes she hiked as straight uphill as she could before catching the trail again farther on. It was slow going. The mountainside was steep and rocky; the tall grasses and scrubby bushes caught at her skirts. Her hands were full of her bag and the lantern, so she couldn't use them to steady herself. Soon she was sweating under her coat, while the brisk breeze still bit at her nose and the bottoms of her earlobes where her hat didn't fully cover. Her fingers were numb from the cold.

After an hour or two, Laurie was beginning to wish she'd asked Mr. Brown for a ride after all, even at the risk of losing her secrecy.

The sky slowly paled to dim gray. Laurie paused and looked back at Haven River Falls spread below her. Martha and Mrs. Brown would be waking soon—if Martha had even bothered to go back to bed—and starting breakfast. She wished she could stay longer with their family. But Laurie didn't allow herself to linger. She turned and continued to climb, determined to make more progress before the sun rose.

The sky lightened so gradually and remained so gray and

CHAPTER 7

overcast that Laurie barely noticed that the day had fully begun. She was grateful for the clouds and hoped that they'd hide her from view. She'd lost track of time, plodding steadily upward, when the sound of hoofbeats broke the silence and shook her to attention. Heart racing, Laurie scurried off the path, diving behind a rock. It was stupid, really—if the rider was coming up the mountain from town, they'd already seen her, and they could see her still if they looked directly at the rock. It wasn't large enough to give her much cover. Laurie's pulse thundered in her ears, keeping time with the hoofbeats, making it difficult for her to ascertain which direction the riders were coming from. She could at least tell that there was more than one horse. She huddled low, holding her breath as the riders passed close, fingering her meager excuse for a defensive weapon—a pocket knife Martha had found for her. No one spoke; no one shouted that they'd found her. The horses continued on, the rumble of hooves fading.

Laurie peeked around the rock and breathed a sigh of relief. It was only one rider leading two packhorses, and they were heading down the mountain. No one had pursued her. Yet.

She scrambled to her feet and continued her climb, colder than ever. The wind whipped harder so high on the mountainside, but Laurie had no choice but to keep going. She ignored the numbness in her nose and fingers, ignored how heavy her legs felt, and tromped onward, determined to get over the pass.

***

John checked the sky as he stepped out of the boarding house and strode toward the mercantile. He was cutting it close: those clouds were getting darker and heavier by the minute, and he had no doubt what was coming. He needed to hurry back to the ranch before he got caught out in the storm. He'd left at dawn, ridden straight for the mercantile, and given the Harrisons his list. They'd promised to get the pack horses loaded up within the hour, so John paid Brown one more visit for a shave and a trim. He didn't know why he bothered—no one but Carlos would see him like this, and he would let his hair grow all winter anyway—but old habits died hard, even after seven years away from well-groomed Boston. No harm in looking like the gentleman his mother raised him to be.

The horses were loaded and ready when he got to the mercantile. Wes Harrison held their heads. John nodded to him and hurried inside to pay for his supplies. Back outside, he hitched up the horses and swung into the saddle.

"Storm's coming," Harrison said. "Better hurry over the pass or you'll be stuck here."

"Not happening." John tipped his hat. "Too much work to do to get snowed out of the ranch."

He turned the horses and headed out of town, back up the mountain they'd just come over. He took them as fast as he dared, not wanting to push the animals too hard but afraid to take it slow. There was no time to waste. It was nearing noon, and the first flurries were starting to drift down.

As John rode, he ran through the chore list for the day. He'd fed the cattle before he left; Carlos was checking the cattle and handling the other animals while he was gone; they'd unload his purchases when he got back, and he'd do one more check of the windows and door of the cabin to make sure it was secure against the storm winds.

John's gaze had fallen on a small figure in the distance for several minutes before he realized what he was looking at. A person walking, hunched against the cold, carrying a carpetbag. A woman, with long skirts whipping around her legs. He noticed when she heard him coming. Her head shot up and whipped around. By then he was coming up beside her, and he could see the relief mixed with fear in her expression.

"Can I help you, ma'am?" John reined in the horses. "Where are you off to?"

"The t-train st-station."

The poor woman was shivering. She turned her face away, looking north. Her hat and scarf were pulled so that they only left a gap for her eyes.

John frowned. "You'll never make it."

She stiffened and half turned to shoot a glare up at him. "You think I c-can't walk that far?"

He was caught by her big brown eyes. "No, ma'am, I think you *could*, but there's a storm coming, and you'll be frozen in a snowdrift long before you reach the station."

She turned away again so that he couldn't see her expression. "I don't have a choice. I need to get on the train. I'll find somewhere to shelter and wait out the storm."

John shook his head. The woman was determined, he'd give her that. But her accent said she was a new arrival from back East, and he'd bet she'd never experienced a snowstorm like this was bound to be.

"I don't know if that would work wherever you're from, ma'am, but that's not the way to survive a storm out here. My place isn't far. I'll give you a ride."

"No, thank you."

"Ma'am, I don't think you realize the danger. I can't leave you to die out here, but if we stay here arguing too much longer, we'll both be caught in the storm." His horse jigged sideways as if impatient for his warm barn and oats. That gave John an idea. "My cabin's snug, and it's got a coal stove that warms it nicely. You'll have the place to yourself—I'll sleep in the barn with my ranch hand. Think about it—food, a fire, a chair, a bed…"

Her shoulders slumped. He could tell she was too weary and cold to argue much longer. "I need to get away," she said, barely louder than a whisper.

John frowned. What in Haven River Falls could be so bad she'd fled into the jaws of a storm?

Chapter 8

"No one's leaving town for a while," the stranger assured Laurie. "Not in this weather. You'll be safe at the ranch."

Laurie studied him. His wool Stetson was pulled low, and the collar of his shearling jacket was flipped up to keep the wind off his neck. Even so, she could see his clean-shaven jaw, clenched strong and unyielding. He had a long nose, not quite too big for his face, and his eyes, what she could see in the shadow of his hat, looked some shade of blue-green. He held her gaze, and his was so forthright that she found she believed him. This man clearly knew the weather out here better than she did, and she was so cold and tired that she didn't know how much longer she'd be able to walk anyway.

"I guess I'll have to trust you," she said.

He gave a nod and dismounted, reaching for her carpetbag. Her fingers were so numb she couldn't even feel him taking it from her hand. She'd considered grabbing for her knife as he'd approached, but she didn't think she could hold it. She watched him strap the bag onto the back of one of the packhorses. She recognized him now as the rider who'd frightened her so badly when he'd passed that morning. He must have gone into town for supplies. He took the lantern, cold and dark now, from her other hand and tucked it among the baggage. Then he turned to her again, studying her for just a second. He was taller than she was but not so much as to be intimidating.

"Beg your pardon, ma'am," he said politely. Then he picked her up by the waist as though she weighed no more than the carpetbag and set her gently on the rolled-up blanket behind the saddle. Before she knew it, he'd mounted in front of her. "Hold tight."

Obediently, Laurie hugged her arms around his waist, though her hands were so cold she couldn't grab onto his coat. He called to the horses, and they were off. Laurie ducked her head against his back to keep out of the wind, resting her icy face against the sheepskin of his coat. She couldn't help noticing that he smelled of outdoors and horses, of hay and hard work and clean sweat. Unbidden, she remembered the unwashed, alcoholic reek of Mr. Knowles, only made worse by the hint of a woman's perfume that clung to him. Already, she felt more at ease with this stranger.

They turned off the track, and Laurie raised her head to look around. Snowflakes nipped at her nose and eyelids, but she managed to glimpse the wooden sign before they passed it—the circled N that Mr. Harrison had told her marked the Newcomb Ranch. Which only made sense, her befuddled brain reminded her: most of the land north of town belonged to the Newcomb spread.

She rested her head forward against her rescuer again, letting his body heat warm her. She ought to remain alert, ready to fight or flee if he turned out to be less trustworthy than she'd guessed. Instead, her mind drifted, nearly to the point of sleep. What a day it had been already, and it was far from over.

CHAPTER 8

***

John pulled the horses to a stop in front of the barn, hollering for Carlos as he dismounted. He turned quickly to catch his passenger, who'd lost her balance when he moved and nearly tumbled from the saddle. He scooped her up in his arms as Carlos emerged from the barn. The cowboy's eyebrows shot upward when he saw what John carried.

"Found her walking. Said she was trying to get to the train station." He shrugged slightly, glancing down at the woman in his arms. Her eyes were open, but she seemed dazed and vague. Her scarf had slipped down her face. He could see the freckles dusting her pale nose and cheeks. "You start unloading while I get her settled, then I'll be back out to help."

Carlos nodded without a word and led the horses into the barn. John turned and crossed to the cabin, shouldering open the door and pushing it closed behind him with one boot. Three long strides brought them to the two rocking chairs set before the coal stove. He settled her into one, then pulled off his gloves and hastened to stoke the fire. He sat back on his heels as he watched the flames grow before closing the door and turning to his guest.

She was looking around with wide eyes, and he was struck again by how pretty those eyes were. Like coffee with cream and sugar, or like freshly made caramels. Sweet and warm. He shook himself and glanced around the cabin, suddenly seeing it as she must. It was one small room, with shelves and a dry sink lining one wall, the stove on another. The ladder to the loft bedroom was on a third wall. Only three small windows punctuated the log walls. A table with a low bench beside it; two rocking chairs. There wasn't a single softening touch in the place, and it had been too long since he'd swept or dusted.

"It's not much," he muttered, warmth creeping into his neck and ears. "Nothing fancy, but it's as airtight as we could make it."

"It's cozy," she said, her voice sleepy and slow like honey.

"Bed's up in the loft. Make yourself at home." He stood up, wishing he could stay inside with her a bit longer. Just to make sure she was alright after being out in the cold so long. Not because she was the first woman he'd seen beyond the ladies at the boarding house or mercantile since he'd settled out here. But snowstorms waited for no one. "Don't leave the house until the storm's good and over. I'll come dig you out."

She blinked at him. He expected her to ask about the weather or where to find something in the house.

Instead, "What's your name?" She tilted her head slightly to the side, and a faint furrow appeared between her brows.

"John Newcomb, ma'am."

"Thank you, Mr. Newcomb." She sat up a little straighter, as if coming back to herself a bit more. "I'm Laurie Kerstetter."

John couldn't stop the smile from tugging at the corners of his mouth. Laurie seemed like just the sort of sweet name for a woman who kept making him think of sugar. Suddenly tongue tied, he touched the brim of his hat, nodded, and made for the door. He paused with his hand on the latch. "I'll be right back with your bag." Then he slipped out and pulled the door tightly closed behind him.

The snow had picked up, already swirling thick and white through the yard. John jogged to the barn and let himself in. Carlos already had the packhorses unloaded, their burdens piled neatly in one corner. Miss Kerstetter's carpetbag sat apart on its own. John scooped it up, said, "Be right back," and

CHAPTER 8

jogged back across the yard.

***

Laurie warmed up gradually along with the cabin. After Mr. Newcomb left her bag just inside the door and cautioned her again not to go outside, she rocked in the chair by the stove as her fingers, toes, nose, and ears ached. The sharp pain shook her from her stupor, and she cautiously peeled back her gloves, wincing, and held her hands out toward the stove. They were red but not frostbitten. That was something to be thankful for. The gloves Beth had given her had done their job. As she grew warmer, she shed her scarf and hat as well, then her coat. She also realized that she was starving. She'd brought some food with her from the boarding house, biscuits and a couple of apples, things that she could sneak out easily and carry in her pockets. But she'd eaten them hours ago. How had she thought it would be enough to last her all the way to the train station, when she was using so much energy walking?

She shook her head. Her plans had been hastily made in desperation, which was never wise. She'd figured that if she could make it to the station, she could either beg the stationmaster and his wife to let her stay with them in their cabin or sleep on the floor of the tiny office until the next eastbound train came through in a few days. And while she hadn't met any of the dangers that a gun would have helped against, she'd failed to predict others. Yet again, her plans had been faulty.

But—by the grace of God and the kindness of a stranger—it had worked out.

She'd made it out of Haven River Falls, and if the weather

and Mr. Newcomb were to be believed, no one would be able to follow her for some time. She was safe and warm for the time being, and it was enough.

Laurie got up from the rocking chair, deciding to explore the kitchen and see what she could find to eat. In jars on the shelves, she found flour, sugar, salt. There were eggs in a basket, and some cans and jars of preserves. As she passed a window, she glanced outside and froze. Everything was white. Snow whirled through the air so thickly that she couldn't see a single thing. Laurie had experienced squalls like this in Pennsylvania, but this went on longer than she'd ever seen. She stood by the window for several long minutes, watching the shifting shades of white, waiting for it to pass, before her stomach reminded her what she'd been doing. She hastily mixed together a pot of porridge on the stove and ate half before it had fully cooled, blowing on it and burning her tongue, but relishing the warmth and fullness in her stomach. Each glance at the window showed that the snow had not abated.

Laurie shivered. Mr. Newcomb had been right—if he hadn't brought her here, she'd likely have died there beside the road.

Shaking off such morbid thoughts, she climbed the ladder to the loft. The angles of the roof made the room one long triangle. A straw tick mattress lay tucked into one of the narrow angles, a wool blanket tucked neatly around it and a folded quilt plopped in the middle. Laurie wondered how often Mr. Newcomb sat up too quickly and hit his head on the low roof. Crates and trunks filled the rest of the small space. Laurie didn't want to pry into Mr. Newcomb's personal things, and the light through the single tiny window was too dim and gray to see much anyway. She did notice a small broom tucked into one corner, though, and carried it downstairs with her. If she was

CHAPTER 8

going to be in his home—while he slept in the barn, no less—she could at least tidy the place up for him.

After sweeping up the main floor of the cabin, Laurie tugged open the door to push the dirt pile outside. The wind whipped the door wide, and she gasped at its icy fingers. She hurriedly swept out the dirt and encroaching snow and slammed the door shut again.

"Should have known better," she chided herself. "You saw what it was like out the window."

But she felt better for having the floor clean, the accomplishment of having done something productive. It was the most she could manage, however. The fatigue from the day caught up with her. She reheated and ate the rest of the porridge, washed the pot with water from the bucket beside the sink, and carried her carpetbag up to the loft. She spread out the quilt over the bed and folded back the blankets then changed into her nightdress. Sliding between the sheets, Laurie snuggled into the little nest. The blankets smelled like Mr. Newcomb's coat had—of horses and outdoors and hard work with a hint of a spicy undertone—reminding her of the awkward fact that she was sleeping in the man's bed. But it couldn't be helped, and she would never allow herself to admit how much she liked the scent.

The snow continued much the same the next day. Laurie almost thought that the flakes weren't falling as fast, but the wind was whirling what had already fallen and drifting it across the yard. Since it didn't look like she'd be leaving the cabin any time soon, Laurie decided to make herself busy. She started by making breakfast, and as she gathered the ingredients to make herself some pancakes, she noticed a trapdoor in the floor. Her curiosity got the better of her, and she left what she was doing to open it and look inside. It was too dark to get a good look, so she climbed down into the small room. After a moment of shivering in the chill air, her vision adjusted to the darkness. She could make out stores of food on shelves and in barrels and crates lining the walls. This must be the root cellar, and if she had to guess, it was about half the size of the cabin, dug into the hard earth and lined with rough field stones. Laurie climbed back into the kitchen, shivering again as the warmer air embraced her. She lowered the trapdoor with a thunk and got back to making breakfast.

She ate and cleaned up, then stood in the kitchen with her hands on her hips, looking around. She wasn't used to idleness. There was always something to do on the farm, and even running Beth's home and business and watching Levi had been enough to keep three women occupied every moment of the day. Just because this wasn't her house didn't mean there weren't chores to be done. She'd already made the bed, cleaned the ashes from the stove and added more coal, and tidied the kitchen. Although… she'd noticed some dust on the shelves, and there were cobwebs in the corners near the ceiling. She could deal with those. She took the broom and batted down the cobwebs then searched for a rag to use for dusting. Nothing came to hand, so Laurie climbed into the loft to look. There must be something in one of the crates. Laurie disturbed as little as she could, but she found a Bible and a current Farmer's Almanac tucked atop an extra quilt in the crate nearest the bed. Another crate along the far wall had some kind of fabric piled in it, and Laurie carried it closer to the window to get a better look. She lifted out the top piece and shook it out. A worn flannel shirt, with holes at the elbows, tears at the seams, and one sleeve hanging almost entirely off.

CHAPTER 8

The sleeve detached with an easy tug. Laurie grinned. This was exactly what she was looking for. This poor shirt had no chance of being mended but would make a perfect cleaning rag.

She set it aside and dug deeper into the crate, finding other pieces of clothing in varying states of disrepair. Some of them simply needed a repaired seam or a patched hole. Some were in too rough a shape to be good for anything but cutting into pieces and using for rags or quilt pieces. One pair of socks had holes at the toes and heels that were beyond hope of darning. Laurie took them back downstairs with her, thinking she could unravel them and reuse the yarn. She wanted to bring the whole crate down, but she didn't think she could manage it on the ladder, so she bundled up a few of the mendable pieces and tucked them under one arm as she descended. She set them on the seat of the second rocking chair, since there was no one else in the cabin to need it, and then set to work dusting the shelves and every surface she could reach with the detached sleeve from the flannel shirt.

As long as she was cleaning, Laurie decided to wash the windows as well. She couldn't wash the outsides of the panes, but she could clean the insides. "Curtains would help," she murmured to herself as she did. "It's a cozy little room, but curtains and a rug would make it feel more like a home." She hadn't found anything in the crate that could be repurposed as window dressings, however, so she let that idea go.

When she'd cleaned all she could think of to clean, Laurie plopped herself in the open rocker and cut patches from a pair of wool trousers that deserved their place in the rag bag—or crate, in this case—and used the material to fix two others. The dark wool was not the same shade; the patches were faded brown while the trousers she was repairing were a darker brown and a navy blue. But they would do for ranch work. Laurie smiled as her hands worked the familiar task. She'd mended more pieces of clothing for Pa and Harvey over the years than she could count. Some of them multiple times, too. She was glad she'd packed her sewing kit when she'd come west and that she'd thought to stock it with full spools of thread. She was grateful for something to do, and more than that, a way to repay Mr. Newcomb for his kindness in letting her stay here to wait out the storm.

Chapter 9

The snow let up enough late in the afternoon for John and Carlos to risk going out. Drifts piled up outside the barn doors so deep that they had to shovel their way through. Once through the worst of the drifts, the snow was only a little over a foot. It made for slow walking, but it wasn't as bad as John had expected. While Carlos continued on to the well to draw water for the herd and to break up the ice on the watering troughs, John returned to the upper floor of the barn and opened the hay door, which allowed him to pitch hay out into the pasture below. The winter pasture, which butted up against the barn, was the only fenced in area on his land besides the horse paddock. Having them near enabled John and Carlos to feed them and keep track of them more easily. Seeking them out on the open range wasn't safe in weather like this.

From his place at the hay door, forking out the last of the evening's hay, John could just barely see his cabin. The windows were dark now, and he supposed Miss Kerstetter had already gone to bed. He hoped she was managing alright on her own in there. But digging her out would have to wait until morning.

Shoveling a path between the barn and the cabin couldn't

even begin the next day until they'd fed and watered the cattle again and milked the two milk cows in the barn. Snow had drifted against the front of the cabin as well so that he had a three-foot pile to shift before he could knock on the door and push it open.

"Sorry it took me so long to get over here, Miss Kerstetter," he said as he kicked snow off his boots before stepping inside and shoving the door shut. The warm air surrounded him like a hug, and with it, the scent of something baking. He looked up, surprised. Nothing that good had ever been smelled in this cabin. His cooking was tolerable, better than George's had been anyway, but this scent went straight to his stomach and made it rumble.

His breath caught as he took in the room, and his hand froze halfway to removing his hat. The young woman who stood by the stove, using a towel to check under the lid of the cast iron dutch oven, looked up at him and smiled. He hadn't gotten a good enough look at her that first day. She was beautiful. Her hair was a warm chestnut, the same sweet-as-coffee-and-cream shade as her eyes, and it was in one long braid that hung over her shoulder. Her smile was bright as summer sunshine, and her lips were a pink that made him think of the peonies his sister used to grow in her garden of pots. She approached him slowly, her smile turning shy. He realized now that she was younger than he'd expected, twenty at most. She wasn't particularly tall, the top of her head coming just about to his mouth, the perfect height for him to press a kiss to her forehead. Not that he was thinking about kissing her. Or he shouldn't be, anyway.

"I hope you didn't rush," she said, her voice still as honey-sweet as he remembered from the other day. "Did the animals all come through the storm alright?"

"They did, thank you, ma'am." Heat rose in the back of John's neck as he found himself stammering. "Have you found everything you needed in here? I don't have much for entertainment."

"Not a problem," she said, grinning and shooting a glance at the chairs beside the stove. One of them appeared to be piled with clothing. "I'm used to keeping busy. I tidied up a bit, and I found some mending that needed doing. I hope you don't mind."

"Mind?" John blinked at her. "That's more than generous of you, Miss Kerstetter."

"Phooey." She brushed it off. "You saved my life. It's the least I could do." Her gaze turned serious as she looked out the nearest window. "You were right about the snow. Thank you."

The heat climbed from John's neck to his ears, and he shrugged. Her gratitude made him feel awkward, so he removed his hat and changed the subject. "What smells so good in here?"

"I wanted to make muffins," Miss Kerstetter said. "I didn't have the right pan, so I guess it's a cake, but made with my mama's muffin recipe." She clasped her hands together behind her and shifted on her feet, appearing as bashful as he was. "If I'm leaving soon to go to the train station, I figured I'd leave you with something sweet."

John's stomach sank. He wasn't surprised that she was ready to move on, but he hated to be the one delivering bad news. "I'm afraid you won't be able to make it to the train station yet, Miss Kerstetter."

"Well, no, I doubt I could walk far in this snow," she agreed, "but when it melts."

"It's not likely to melt until spring."

"Spring?" Her big eyes widened.

"Winter here isn't like wherever you're from," he reminded her.

"Pennsylvania," she said softly.

He nodded. "If the winters there were anything like what I grew up with in Massachusetts, I can safely say that you can expect winter here in Wyoming to be colder and snowier than anything you've seen. Probably longer, too."

"So the train station…"

"Is beyond our reach for the time being." The horses and sleigh could make it, of course, but John couldn't spare them from the ranch work for the full day it would take. And the trail wasn't well marked. With snow covering the wheel ruts, there would be no way to keep to the path and avoid getting lost.

"And Haven River Falls?"

"That snow will have closed the pass. No one's getting to or from town until everything melts."

***

Laurie felt like Mr. Newcomb had dumped a bucket of ice water over her. Once again, her plans were proven to be ill-conceived. She shivered and hugged her arms around herself, her mind turning over the new revelations. On the one hand, she didn't need to worry about Mr. Knowles coming after her. She had months before she risked facing him again, and hopefully the way to the train station would clear long before the pass. On the other hand, she was stuck here, reliant again on someone's hospitality, and this time it was a stranger rather

CHAPTER 9

than a friend. A very handsome stranger, whose blue-green eyes were studying her with concern. What would Pa say if he knew the predicament Laurie had gotten herself into?

Laurie's throat closed, and tears threatened to spill at the thought. Pa would never have let her come west at all, not without either himself or Harvey accompanying her until they were certain she was happily settled. But Pa was gone, which was the only reason she'd left the farm in the first place. His loss grated on her heart, leaving her insides rough and raw.

She swallowed hard and blinked away the tears, avoiding Mr. Newcomb's eyes. She'd done so well at pushing down her emotions and only letting them out when she was alone. Even Beth and Essie hadn't seen her cry since the funeral.

"Oh no." Beth. Essie. They were expecting letters from her. Harvey and Mary. The last they knew, she'd boarded a train to come out West. "We can't get letters out, can we?"

Mr. Newcomb shook his head.

Laurie bit the side of her lip. "Harvey's going to kill me," she muttered.

Mr. Newcomb scowled. "No one will hurt you. Who's Harvey?"

"Oh, not like that," Laurie hastened to reassure him. "He's my cousin back in Pennsylvania. He's probably already furious with me for running off like I did without warning. If he doesn't hear from me for months…"

His expression softened. "I truly am sorry, but there's no help for it." He studied her for a moment. "I hate to pry, but if this Harvey fellow isn't why you left Haven River Falls… What are you running from? Don't feel you have to tell me. I just… It would help me to know what I might need to protect you from."

A weight settled in Laurie's stomach. She wished she could

forget all about Mr. Knowles and never admit her folly to another soul, but Mr. Newcomb had earned a right to know. "I… I replied to an advertisement for a bride," she said, cheeks flaming. "I never promised anything, but after a few letters, I decided that I needed to meet him and see the town in person. As it turned out, the letters were nothing but lies that he'd had one of the saloon girls write for him." Her mouth twisted at the sour words. "He… didn't take kindly to my reluctance, and…" She didn't want to repeat the threat he'd made, to have her with or without the preacher's blessing. It made her feel cheap to even have such a thing suggested of her.

Mr. Newcomb's face darkened as he listened. "Who was it?" There was a hint of a growl to his voice, and it sent a shiver through Laurie.

"Todd Knowles."

A flash of recognition and a tightening of his jaw were his only reaction.

"Martha Brown helped me sneak out," Laurie continued, hugging herself tighter, as if her arms could hold the rest of her together. "I promised to write to her, too, to let her know I was safe."

"Sounds like you've got a whole passel of people worrying about you, Miss Kerstetter," he said, still frowning but with a gentler tone. "But *you* don't need to worry. You're safe here."

"Thank you." Laurie suddenly felt awkward standing just a few feet from him, the snow melting off his boots onto the floor. She backed a little farther toward the stove. "The muffin cake should be ready in a quarter hour or so, if you're hungry. And I'll make dinner tonight. There's just the two of you, right?"

"You don't need to do that."

"I want to. It will give me something to do, and I'll be glad of the company."

"We'd be most obliged." He put his hat back on, tipped it to her, and let himself out of the cabin.

Laurie checked the cake again, then lit a candle and carried it down to the root cellar to gather supplies for the evening meal. She spent the afternoon alternating between cooking and mending. The sun had gone down, and she'd found candles to light on the table by the time the knock came on the door.

"Come in," she called out.

The door opened, and Mr. Newcomb entered, followed by another man. Laurie watched as they both shucked off their coats and hats and hung them on hooks by the door.

"Do you mind taking off your boots too?" she asked. "It'll save me cleaning later." She knew from her own experience that the planed wood floor was impressively smooth and splinter-free.

Mr. Newcomb nodded at his ranch hand, and they both toed off their boots and approached the table in their socks. Laurie noticed that the rancher had shaved since she'd seen him at noon. Before, he'd been sporting a few days' dark stubble that made him look even more rugged and quintessentially western. She liked both looks on him. He looked younger without the shadow along his jaw, though, and she realized that he couldn't be much older than her cousin.

He introduced his ranch hand as Carlos Vasquez. Mr. Vasquez was swarthy and only about Laurie's height, much closer to five feet than six. His hair was darker than Mr. Newcomb's ordinary brown, and his beard already looked like it had been growing for a few weeks. Despite this, Laurie guessed that he was young, no older than his boss. She had been nervous as she prepared dinner at the thought of meeting another cowboy; Mr. Knowles wasn't the most encouraging example of the profession. But Mr. Newcomb had assured her that she was safe here, and she trusted him. And she was immediately set at ease when Mr. Vasquez responded to her smile of welcome with a broad, friendly grin of his own, which crinkled the corners of his eyes and made her feel that they could very easily be friends.

"Have a seat." Laurie gestured to the table where she'd set out three plates. She'd dragged one of the rocking chairs over so that the men could share the bench on one side and she could sit in the chair opposite them. She'd left the stack of mended and folded clothes on the seat so that she could gain a few extra inches and see more easily over the table. It wasn't ideal, but it would do for tonight.

While they took their places, she uncovered the food she'd already set out—cold potato salad, green beans, rolls—and brought over the plate of sliced ham she'd left on the stove to keep warm. They all had water to drink, as Laurie hadn't found anything else but milk in the cellar.

Mr. Newcomb looked into his cup with a frown. "Sorry, Miss Kerstetter. We took all the coffee out to the barn so we could make it as we start chores in the mornings. Helps to keep warm, you know? I didn't think to leave some inside for you. I'll bring some over first thing."

She shook her head. "I don't drink it much anyway. Keep it out there, and if I want some, I know where to find it." She gave him a small smile and took a bite of potato.

Mr. Vasquez, already nearly halfway done his plate, paused and took a long drink. "The food's mighty good, Miss Kerstetter."

"Thank you, Mr. Vasquez."

"Call me Carlos, ma'am. I don't reckon I can go the whole

winter being called mister like some hoity-toity city fella."

Laurie laughed. "If you insist. Have you lived out here long?"

"Been here going on two years. Before that I wrangled cattle all over but never found a place I wanted to stay more than a season or two." He took another bite, and around the food, he explained, "I'm originally from California. All my family are *vaqueros*—cowboys."

Laurie remembered the look her mother used to give when she or Harvey used to speak with their mouth full at the table. She bit back a chuckle, imagining herself using the same look on Carlos. Manners were probably often forgotten when it was just men living together on the back edge of civilization.

She turned to Mr. Newcomb. "And how long have you been out West? You said you were from New England?"

"Yes, ma'am, Boston." He gulped down the bite he'd just taken and took a sip of water. "I came west seven years ago with my brother George. And though I am a 'city fella'—" he grinned at Carlos—"you can call me John. No need to be stuffy when we'll be sharing the ranch all winter."

Laurie felt her face heat. Mama would have insisted on the proper forms of address, but Mr. Newcomb made a point. And they were in the uncivilized West, after all.

She smiled. "Then you both may call me Laurie. Now that's settled, John, how did you find yourself in Haven River Falls?"

He shrugged. "We came out on the train to Cheyenne and started asking around about land for sale. We heard about a family wanting to sell out and move to Cheyenne, so we made a deal and were out here only a few days later. We started with a herd of twenty-five."

"How many do you have now?" Laurie asked.

"Nearing four hundred."

Laurie's eyes widened. "That's a lot of cattle for two people to look after. Where's your brother now?"

John's expression froze, and he looked down at his plate, stabbing at a green bean. Something in Laurie recognized his emotion without being able to put it into words. She wished she hadn't said anything, even before he answered. "He died two years ago. Accident with a bull."

"I'm sorry," she whispered.

He nodded once without raising his eyes and began eating again. Laurie took a bite of her roll, which was now dry and tasteless. She regretted her questions, though she had been making innocent conversation. His pain only reminded her of her own loss. She took a drink of water to wash down the roll, followed by a few slow breaths, willing the tightness around her chest to ease and the burning in her eyes to recede.

When the silence had stretched on a little too long, and John showed no signs of looking up from his plate, Laurie asked Carlos if he would tell her about California. "I've lived in Pennsylvania all my life," she said. "The only other parts of the country I've seen are what passed the train window."

The cowboy cheerfully told her about the places he'd seen—the mining towns and ghost towns, the port of San Francisco and the vineyards farther north. John relaxed as the conversation moved on, enough to meet Laurie's eyes a couple of times, though he didn't volunteer any more personal details.

They finished up the meal with the muffin cake Laurie had made earlier. Before they left for the barn, John gathered a few more of his things from the loft. He pulled on his boots and coat in silence, and then, after Carlos had said a friendly goodnight and stepped out into the cold, he paused beside the door.

CHAPTER 9

"Thanks for dinner, Miss Kerstetter. Laurie." Laurie thought she saw a blush turning his ears red, but it was hard to tell in the candlelight. "It was delicious."

"I'm glad you liked it. We've enough rolls and ham left to have sandwiches for lunch tomorrow," she offered. "And I'm thinking of making stew for dinner." He opened his mouth to protest, but she stopped him. "I've been cooking for my father and cousin every day for years. I wouldn't know what to do with myself if you didn't let me cook."

He blinked at her, as if he'd never seen such a perplexing creature, before smiling. "Well, then, thank you. Have a good night, ma'am."

"You too." She watched him leave, smiling to herself as she turned to clean up the kitchen before making her way to bed.

Chapter 10

Laurie was awake with the dawn, habit bolstered by the fact that the single window in the loft faced east. The sun rose brilliantly into what soon became the bluest sky Laurie had ever seen. The light gleamed off the snow so brightly it hurt to look at. Laurie scrambled into her clothes, the chilly morning air waking her up even more thoroughly than the light. She lit a fire in the stove, then breakfasted on leftover cake before pulling on her boots, coat, and accessories. Farm work always started early, and a ranch was just a different type of farm. She had a couple of hours before she needed to start the stew for dinner, so she'd find something useful to do.

Despite the ostentatious sun, the air was icy. Laurie hurried to the barn, barely opening the creaking door wide enough to slip through before she closed it against the chill. There was a wide aisle between lines of stalls on either side, and an open space in the middle with a cast-iron stove. Neither rancher nor cowboy was anywhere in sight.

"Good morning," she called.

A quickly muffled curse sounded from a stall somewhere to the right, and a hatted head peered over a stall door to the left. Carlos waved to her and called a good morning, gesturing to the kettle on the small stove and offering her coffee.

CHAPTER 10

"No thanks," she said. "I've come to help with chores."

Carlos stared at her. Laurie wondered briefly if she'd accidentally spoken in tongues. Then John—no longer cursing, but now using a rag to wipe his hands—emerged from another stall with a bucket of milk. He set it in the aisle and bent to wipe the top of one boot. If Laurie had to guess, she'd probably startled him into missing the pail.

He approached her slowly, his gaze taking her in from head to toe, and Laurie felt suddenly self-conscious. She tucked her gloved hands into her coat pockets so that she wouldn't fiddle with the buttons or the ends of her scarf. He stopped several feet away, cramming his own hands into pockets.

"What can I help you with, ma'am?"

"Nothing," she said. "I was hoping I could help you."

Carlos was still leaning over the stall door, watching.

"We're just letting the horses outside before we feed the cattle," John said. Carlos's hat disappeared, and a second later he opened the stall door and led a horse out and down the aisle toward them. "The haymow isn't a place for a lady. It's dirty and dangerous."

Laurie frowned. She wanted to argue that she was perfectly capable of the work, but John Newcomb probably knew more about this than she did, just like he'd been right about the weather. Wyoming was different than Pennsylvania, and this was a ranch. Pa hadn't had hay or cattle. They'd farmed corn in addition to their subsistence garden and Laurie's goats.

"Fair enough," she said, meeting his gaze square on. "But you can't tell me that's the only chore there is to do. I've lived all my life on a farm. I can gather eggs, milk cows, muck stalls…"

She raised an eyebrow in challenge, though the effect might have been lost because of how low her hat was pulled against the cold. "Give me a quick tour of the barn, and I'll get to work while you deal with the cattle."

Once again, Laurie got the impression that she baffled her host. What kind of women had he been used to in Boston? Or had he simply been in the predominantly male West for so long that he'd forgotten how resilient women were?

He rubbed the back of his neck and shook his head as if bewildered. "I've already done the milking," he muttered.

"Do you have chickens?" she prompted.

"Yes, ma'am." With a sigh, he waved her forward into the barn, leading her past Carlos and the horse he was waiting to take outside. The cowboy winked at her, which startled Laurie, but it was more as if they were sharing a joke and not inappropriate or flirtatious. She wondered if he found it amusing to see his boss flustered.

The barn was built with sixteen stalls, eight on either side of the aisle. Half were occupied by horses. The one nearest the stove had bedrolls, folded buffalo robes, and piles of what looked like personal belongings. Laurie turned away quickly from what must be where the men slept. John told her that the three empty stalls were kept in case any of the cows calved early, so that mamas and babies could be in where it was warm rather than out in the bitter cold and deep snow. Two more housed the milk cows, and one was piled high with clean hay so that they didn't need to bring it down from the mow every day. The final stall had been fitted with rows of nest boxes and surrounded by wire fencing, containing a small flock of chickens. At the far end of the barn was a storage room for horses' tack, tools, chicken feed, and sundry other things.

"I haven't dealt with the chickens yet," he said, frowning into the indoor coop. "The horses have been fed, but the stalls aren't

CHAPTER 10

done."

His reluctance to tell her was so obvious that Laurie almost laughed. "I'll start with the chickens," she said, thinking he'd object less to her feeding the birds and collecting eggs than he would to letting her muck out stalls. She intended to do all of it, whatever she could to help, but she might as well ease him into it. She'd spent long enough feeling like she was mooching off Beth's hospitality; she intended to work just as hard here so that she earned her keep.

He touched his fingers to the brim of his Stetson, the barest tip of his hat in acknowledgement. Then he followed Carlos, who had returned to lead out another horse, and the two men went about their own work. Laurie could hear their muffled voices speaking from the haymow overhead but couldn't make out their words. She scooped out feed corn for the chickens, luring them from their nests so that she could easily collect their eggs. She set the basket of eggs in the aisle out of the way, then she cleaned the coop stall as best she could. At home, she would have let the chickens outside to forage while she cleaned their space, but not in snow this deep.

By the time she was done, Laurie's fingers were going numb. Her nose ached with cold, and she had been ignoring her shivers for several minutes. The stove in the center of the aisle was too small to bring much heat to the space. Laurie scooped up the basket of eggs and pail of milk and hurried back to the cabin, heaving a sigh of relief as she pushed the door shut. The warmth of the cabin slowly seeped into her, and she stood by the stove for a minute before taking off her outerwear. She probably ought to have waited for the men to return so that she could tell them that she'd only cared for the chickens, but they hadn't returned to the barn by the time she was finished, and she was too cold to wait around. Once she started the stew cooking, she'd go back out.

***

John was relieved to see that Laurie had gone back to the cabin before they returned from tending the cattle. She'd fed the chickens and cleaned the coop, but a glance at Star's empty stall showed him that she hadn't done any mucking. Good. She was a guest, if a reluctant one. Just cooking for them was more than he'd ever ask.

He and Carlos fell into their familiar routine of one of them cleaning the stalls while the other brought the horses in from the pasture. They couldn't let them stay out too long in this weather, and they'd already been out a while.

John had just set the pitchfork aside from spreading the last of the clean hay and dusted off his hands when the door to the barn opened. He expected Carlos and opened his mouth to tell his friend that the last stall was done. But though the figure was the same height as Carlos, it definitely wasn't the stocky cowboy.

Even bundled in her coat and knitwear, Laurie Kerstetter was so pretty he couldn't help staring. The brilliant midday sunlight from outside lit her from behind, giving her a kind of angelic glow. She turned to slide the door shut, returning the barn to peaceful dimness and giving him the chance to take a breath and pick his jaw up off the floor. He mentally kicked himself. Why did he have to turn dopey every time he saw her?

Bracing himself, he turned to face her. She carried a basket in front of her, whatever was inside it covered in a clean towel. He didn't recognize the basket, but there were a lot of things

CHAPTER 10

in the kitchen that he had never used—when they'd bought the homestead, it had come with the house and barn and everything in them.

"I wasn't sure when you'd have a moment to eat," she said, coming to stand in front of him and gesturing with the basket. "I made ham sandwiches with the leftovers from dinner."

"Thank you." He smiled, and his heart leapt when she responded in kind. "We just need to wash up. You're in perfect time."

She glanced into the nearest stalls, noticing for the first time that they were clean. Her face fell. "I was going to help with those," she said. "I just needed to get dinner on the stove."

John's sense of victory at finishing the task before she could attempt it was tempered by the disappointment on her face. "You've already helped a lot by caring for the chickens and feeding us," he said gently.

She pursed her lips but merely nodded. She set down the basket on a wooden stool near the stove and headed for the door. "Dinner will be ready at sundown," she said. And then she was gone.

John couldn't figure why she would even *want* to muck stalls. His experience with women was mostly limited to Missy and her friends, and he couldn't imagine a single one of them being disappointed at missing out on such a dirty, smelly job. He couldn't picture one of them even entering a working barn on purpose, let alone volunteering to help. He finally shook his head, bewildered, and went to help Carlos bring the last two horses back in from the cold.

Laurie came out to the barn even earlier the next morning. Carlos was starting the coffee on the stove while John fed the horses. They'd take Crescent and Milky Way to check the cattle and the pasture fence line this morning. He made sure to alternate which horses came out with them so that they all got a fair balance of exercise and rest. Everyone worked harder in the summer when the cattle were out on the open range, but even in winter everyone did their part.

Laurie greeted both men with a smile and wished them good morning, coming close to where John stood inside Crescent's stall. The quarter horse lowered his head to investigate this new person, and she reached up to stroke the big animal's nose.

"Aren't you beautiful?" she murmured.

"That's Crescent," John said. "I also have his brother Star." He gestured to the next stall. Both horses were brown with white on their faces and chests, vaguely in the shapes they were named for.

She smiled. "Good morning, Crescent. I hope you're ready for a cold day because it's chilly out there."

Carlos chuckled from farther down the aisle. "That sums up winter in Wyoming, ma'am."

She laughed, and John both enjoyed the sound and felt a twinge of jealousy that he wasn't the one who caused it. He eased out of Crescent's stall and moved toward the milk cows, hands in pockets. "If you're here to do chores again, you're welcome to start with the milking. Andie's gonna be fit to burst if she waits much longer."

"Andie?" She followed him.

"Andromeda." He gestured to the cow in the first stall. "Most of our critters are named for stars and such. George named them. He—" Even two years later, his voice caught when he mentioned his brother. "He loved astronomy. That's part of why he loved this land so much—you can see more stars than you ever could guess existed."

CHAPTER 10

He felt a light pressure on his forearm and glanced down. Laurie had rested a gloved hand on his sleeve, and his gaze darted to hers.

"I'm sorry," she said softly. "I… I lost my father just this spring."

It was a simple statement, but it held a world of meaning. She understood. She saw his grief, though it lay buried deep, and she accepted it. That understanding seemed to forge a connection between them, an invisible link that remained even after she removed her hand from his arm. John couldn't find a single word to say, so he just nodded.

"What's the other cow's name?"

"Cass. Cassiopeia." He gave a wry half smile. He knew how ridiculous it sounded to give milk cows such fancy names.

Laurie grinned.

While she got to work milking the two cows, John and Carlos headed out with the cattle. By the time they'd returned, she had finished the milking and had fed both cows and chickens and gathered the eggs.

"If you'll give me a pitchfork, I can start on Crescent's stall," she called as John slid open the barn door.

Something in her voice didn't sound right, and he strode through the barn toward her, his eyes slowly adjusting from the brightness outside.

"What?" she asked. "I found the wheelbarrow."

She had. She'd moved it from the empty stall where they kept it to the aisle. But that wasn't what brought on his frown. "What are you still doing out here? You're freezing."

Her jaw trembled as she tried to stop her teeth from chattering. Her nose and cheeks were pink from the combination of cold air and hard work, and he couldn't help thinking she looked adorable like that. But she was not dressed for this kind of cold.

"I'll be fine. The work warms me up."

"Not enough. Come on." He scooped up the pail of milk. "Grab the eggs, we'll take these inside."

He'd figured enough to know that his only hope of getting her inside where it was warm was to use work as an excuse. She'd stand there arguing until her lips turned blue if he continued to tell her outright. Not that he should be thinking about her lips.

They crossed the yard quickly and tromped into the house, stomping the snow off their boots.

"You could really do with a mat inside the door," she said, her teeth chattering so badly that the words were barely recognizable.

"Sure could," John agreed, setting down the milk and pulling off his gloves. "That something you could make?"

She nodded. He took the egg basket from her unresisting fingers, then reached for her gloves, easing them from her hands finger by finger. Her skin was like ice. He sandwiched her hands between his to warm them up, though his were cold too. That didn't matter to him, not once he discovered just how small and perfect her hands felt. Her skin was calloused from years of work, and he wondered at the stories behind the few small white scars that marked her fingers. Probably minor things, like an accidental cut from a knife while cooking, but he was curious about all of it.

"Need help with your boots?"

"Not if I'm going right back out to the barn."

"You're not," he said firmly. "I've got something to show you in here first."

CHAPTER 10

She raised an eyebrow at him, but she bent and stiffly unlaced her boots. He toed his own boots off, and together they moved toward the stove. They stood and held their hands out to the heat for a silent few minutes. John snuck glances at her, waiting for her shivering to subside and her teeth to stop chattering.

At length, she said, "What was it you wanted to show me?"

Her voice had lost the tremble, so he stepped back from the stove. "Come with me." He led the way up the ladder to the loft. The trunk he wanted was at the foot of the bed, tucked as far into the angle beneath the roof as it could fit. He dragged it out and lifted the lid. He'd thought that seeing George's clothes again would be painful, and it was, but it was a duller ache than he'd expected. It was one of the first lessons one learned when living out here, where supplies were hard to come by: keep everything. Most things could be reused, repaired, or repurposed. He and George had been nearly the same size, and he'd already had to take a few of his brother's clothes when his own had worn out.

George's shearling coat was folded right on top, and John lifted it out. "This should be big enough to fit right over your coat." He held it up in front of her.

She took it, sliding her arms into the sleeves. They were too long, and she had to pause and roll them up a few inches before she could button it. She looked like a child playing dress-up, but it would keep her warm.

John lowered the lid again and shoved the trunk back. "You're welcome to anything else you need in that trunk, and whatever else is here," he added, gesturing to the rest of the loft.

Her big, caramel eyes caught and held his. "Thank you."

He nodded, tipped his hat, which he'd forgotten to take off, and descended the ladder. She followed. They put their boots and gloves back on. John wanted to convince her to stay in the house, but he wasn't sure how. When she'd silently accompanied him all the way back to the barn, he sighed.

"How about I clear out the stalls and you bring in the clean hay?"

A compromise was the best he could think to do. He could see the smile in her eyes even though her scarf was pulled all the way up over her nose.

"That'll work," she said.

He grinned and pulled up his own muffler.

They worked well together, finding a rhythm as natural as he had with Carlos, who was already out with the horses. Laurie hummed as she worked, and he thoroughly enjoyed the sound. They were in the last two stalls when Carlos led the first two horses back inside. John glanced at his friend then looked away, heat rising in his neck. The cowboy's bandana pulled up over his face didn't completely hide his knowing smirk.

Chapter 11

The next week passed in the same way. Laurie rose early and ate quickly, just as she'd been in the habit of doing at home. She bundled up in both coats and went out to the barn to help with the chores. The two milk cows, Andie and Cass, had accepted her presence willingly enough, and the chickens greeted her eagerly every morning when she brought their feed. The men usually returned from feeding and watering the cattle around the same time she finished, and they worked together to care for the horses. Then Laurie went back into the cabin to warm up and spend the rest of the day cooking, cleaning, and mending. John and Carlos rode back out to check the cattle and fences and attend to the other tasks involved in running a ranch. Laurie wasn't certain what all those tasks were, but they kept the men busy. Not so busy, however, that they couldn't pause to eat whatever lunch she brought out for them, or that John couldn't take a minute to shave when he washed up to come in for dinner.

The sky stayed a bright, clear blue, and when Laurie looked out the loft window at night after blowing out her candle, she could see a billion stars scattered across the sky like a dusting of diamonds.

Then came a day when the clouds hung low, heavy, and gray

when Laurie went out to help with the chores.

"Snow's coming," John said, looking up at the sky as he led one of the horses, a pale gray mare called Moonbeam, past Laurie out the barn door. He paused and held her eyes. "If snow starts falling, you stay in the cabin just like last time, alright?"

Laurie remembered how the snow had blustered around the house and fallen so thickly that she couldn't see out the windows. She had no desire to get caught in weather like that. "You'll come dig me out after?"

He nodded, smiled slightly, and led Moonbeam outside.

The expected snow came that night. When Laurie woke the next morning, the windows were a blur of white. "Looks like I'm not helping with chores today," she said to herself. "What shall I do instead?"

The cabin was already tidy. She wouldn't cook any big fancy meals just for herself. Most of the mending was done already. But there was plenty of material in the crate she'd nicknamed the rag bag, and she could use some of that to make a rug to put by the front door.

She pieced scraps together, weaving them into a simple rectangle and tying the ends in place. She liked how it looked when she placed it on the floor—cozy, homelike. It made the space feel more lived-in.

She missed the old farmhouse she'd grown up in. Mama had sewn curtains for every window and quilts for each bed. There were pillows on the sofa and rugs on the wood floor. It was bigger than John's cabin, three bedrooms upstairs and the parlor, kitchen, and Pa's study downstairs. But somehow it had always seemed full of warmth and life, especially when they would bring out the decorations for Christmas. Each

CHAPTER 11

year they'd hung bows and wreaths and paper snowflakes and garlands of popcorn. Laurie had none of those things here, but Christmas would be coming in a few weeks. How would they celebrate it? Last year around this time, she'd been rushing to sew new flannel shirts as gifts for Pa and Harvey, and she'd knit a little romper for baby Levi. This year, she was hundreds of miles away from her family and friends without even the chance to send a letter, let alone gifts.

"Homesick moping won't do anyone any good," she chided herself when the first tear escaped and ran down her cheek. She swiped it away. "Best find some work to do."

So she decided to bake a loaf of bread. As she kneaded the dough, she thought about the holidays. Christmas would certainly look different this year, with no visit to church and no familiar faces and much more snow than she was used to. But there were no restrictions on where joy could be found, and she was among friends here too. As she thought about the men hunkering out with the animals in the barn, ideas began to rise for things she could make as gifts, small things. Once she set the dough by the stove to rise, she cleaned her hands and got started.

Carlos wore his bandana over his face to protect from cold and wind and dust, but it was just thin cambric fabric, light enough to serve the same purpose against dust and wind during the summer. He needed a proper muffler like John had. She didn't have the yarn to knit one, but she could sew one from scraps of flannel, which would be warm but still thin enough that he could breathe through it when he pulled it over his face.

For John, Laurie would unravel the socks that had been too far gone to darn and reknit them so that he'd have a new, warm pair. It wasn't the most exciting thing, but she'd been raised with practical gifts, and somehow she thought he'd appreciate any care and effort on his behalf.

With those plans in place, Laurie got to work, glad of something to occupy her while the snow still swirled outside.

The snow ended midmorning the next day. The path to the barn was only ankle deep, so Laurie made her way across the yard. She found a pail of milk and a basket of eggs sitting in the aisle where they'd been left after morning chores. She carried them back to the house, then found the shovel and cleared the path, her attention drifting like the clouds that were making way for the blue sky to break through.

She ran smack into John when she took the shovel back to the barn.

"I was just looking for that," he said, steadying her with his hands on her arms.

She stood frozen, staring up at him. How had she forgotten how handsome he was in one day apart? But those blue-green eyes were impossible to look away from, and the rough stubble on his jaw was just so intriguing. What was happening to her? When had she started caring about facial hair?

"Why did you need the shovel?"

His voice snapped her out of her stupor. "To clear the path to the cabin," she said, stepping out of his grasp and holding the tool out to him.

He took it, looking at it with a bemused frown. "That's what I was going to do. You beat me to it."

Laurie shrugged. "You beat me to my chores." His eyes darted to hers at the word "my," and she wondered for a second if he'd have a problem with that tiny claim of ownership.

Instead, his mouth ticked up in a smile. "I think Andie and Cass are starting to like you better than me."

CHAPTER 11

Laurie laughed. "Did they tell you so?"

"Andie tried to kick the bucket over twice, and I'm pretty sure Cass was egging her on."

"At least they gave you milk. I'm thinking of making bread pudding tonight."

He grinned. "Can't wait. We sure missed your cooking yesterday."

Laurie returned to the house with a smile on her face and a warm feeling inside. She didn't feel so much like a mooch or an uninvited guest when she knew she was appreciated.

The men knocked and entered just as Laurie set dinner on the table. She'd made a roast with root vegetables cooked alongside and a pudding from the last of the day-old bread. They both remarked on the new rug, careful to kick the snow from their boots and remove them at the door. As they approached the candle-lit table, Laurie noticed that John had shaved again. She glanced between him and Carlos, whose beard hadn't stopped growing since she'd arrived. Something fluttered inside her at the realization that John Newcomb shaved to be presentable for her. Maybe it was the rancher's city upbringing. But he hadn't shaved during either snowstorm when the weather had kept them apart.

"You don't have to shave if you'd rather not," she said, wishing she could stop the blush from warming her cheeks. "I won't be offended, and I expect a beard would be warmer."

"It is," Carlos said, with a grin at John. He took his seat at the table.

The rancher shot his friend a glare before sitting too. "I'd hate for you to think we're all uncouth wild men out here."

Carlos chuckled, knowing the dig was aimed at him.

Laurie laughed. "I don't mind."

***

John looked forward to mornings more than he ever used to. The cold was just as biting, the work just as hard, but then he'd hear Laurie's sweet voice calling a hello, and it was immediately the best day ever. He loved the satisfied almost-smile that flitted across her face when she saw his unshaved jaw. It was still only a few days' worth of scruff. He hadn't at all minded giving up shaving with icy cold water, though he'd gladly keep doing it to look his best for her. But if it made her happy for him to stop, then he wouldn't complain.

He did his best to hide how he lit up when she was around. Carlos saw through him anyway, of course. They'd been living and working together for two years now, and the man was the best friend he'd had since coming west. That was inconvenient now, though. As soon as they were out of earshot of the barn, Carlos teased him.

"You going to spend the whole winter making cow eyes at her?"

"I haven't been—" he protested, then sighed. Lying wouldn't do any good. "Think she's noticed?"

"Nope, she's been too busy doing the same to you."

His heart leapt. "You think so?"

Carlos laughed, a chuckle at first that built into a full belly laugh. He clapped John on the shoulder. "*Hombre*, you're so far gone you couldn't find your way back with a map."

John scowled. His friend was probably right, but he didn't want to admit it. Falling in love with Laurie Kerstetter wasn't the smartest idea. As soon as spring melted the snow, she'd be on a train back to Pennsylvania. Falling for her would only leave him with a broken heart. But his rational mind appeared

CHAPTER 11

to have lost all say in the matter.

One morning, a few days before Christmas, she entered the barn with her usual cheerful greetings followed with, "I'm going to do some laundry today. If you have anything you want washed, can you bring it to the cabin?"

John was in Star's stall, and he stood gaping as she walked to the storage room and returned lugging a big wooden tub. She set it by the barn door and straightened. "Mind bringing this along too?" She shot him a bright smile, and he nodded. He'd agree to just about anything when she smiled at him like that.

He left Star with a pat on the neck. "Be right back," he murmured to the horse.

Then he gathered his spare clothes, dumping them into the tub as Carlos did the same. Laurie was already in Cass's stall, and he could hear the milk hitting the side of the metal bucket in a soft hiss. Carlos glanced back toward the cow's stall, then leaned closer.

"Convince her to stay," he said under his breath. Then he straightened, winked, and went to pick up where John had left off with Star.

Could he? Carlos had been teasing, joking about how much easier a woman made life on the ranch. But could John convince her not to go back East? She'd come to Wyoming with the intention of marrying, after all, so she couldn't be wholly opposed to the idea. He'd have to win her over, court her and woo her, which he had no idea how to do. He'd flirted with a few girls back in Boston, but that was the extent of his experience, and George hadn't set a helpful example as a confirmed footloose bachelor.

Well, he had the rest of winter to figure it out. It was his only hope to keep his heart intact come spring.

***

On Christmas, Laurie cooked ham and mashed potatoes, peas and carrots, and fresh bread, with an apple pie to finish it off. John had shaved again, and both men were dressed in the clothes she'd just washed a few days ago. They all sat together at the table, and before they ate, John read the Christmas story from the Gospel of Luke. Laurie remembered Pa reading aloud from the family Bible, and she wondered if Harvey would read it to Mary. She barely heard half the words as she fought back the tears that swelled any time she thought of Pa.

The sound of a throat clearing brought her back to the moment. Carlos's gaze was on his plate, but John was looking directly at her, sympathy in those beautiful eyes.

"Shall we pray?" he asked gently.

Laurie nodded and bowed her head, and he said a blessing over the food.

Serving and eating brought a welcome distraction, and she was beaming from their compliments by the time the pie was done.

She shyly brought out their gifts. "They're not much, just what I could remake, but there ought to be gifts on Christmas." She shrugged, blushing.

Carlos immediately wrapped his new scarf around his neck so exuberantly that the end of it smacked John in the face. Everyone laughed, and Laurie was grateful for his playful spirit. John himself didn't say much, but she saw how he ran his fingers over the lines of stitches in the socks she'd knit. His expression was a hard-to-read mix of emotions, but she thought overall he was pleased.

When evening fell and the two men put on their coats and

boots, John lingered, letting Carlos leave first.

"I, um…" He rubbed the back of his neck with one hand and fingered something in his pocket with the other. "I have a gift for you too." His eyes met hers, and his ears went an even deeper pink than she'd seen them before. He pulled his hand from his pocket and held out a round gray rock, less than two inches across, that had been chiseled and polished into the shape of a rose with petals wide open. "I found it years ago while I was putting up the pasture fence. No idea where it came from."

Laurie took the stone from him and turned it over in her hands, admiring the work. "It's beautiful," she said.

He lowered his head so that his hat brim hid his face. "Thought you might like it. Merry Christmas." He ducked out the door.

Laurie stood where she was, staring at the spot he'd just vacated. Her fingers traced the contours of the stone rose. Why did it feel like there was an extra weight of significance to that short and seemingly simple interaction?

Chapter 12

The next storm came in early January. Though the morning started out sunny, the temperature dropped steeply as the day went on. At nightfall, Laurie huddled under the blankets, shivering, unable to sleep. She finally gave up on the bed and carried the quilt and wool blanket down the ladder to sleep by the stove. She added more coal, hoping that John and Carlos were warm enough in the barn. All the animals together should produce enough body heat to keep the barn from dropping to an unsafe temperature. She promised herself she'd ask in the morning when she went out to do chores. But now that she was a little warmer, she dropped off to sleep despite lying on the hard floor.

The next morning, however, Laurie couldn't go to the barn for chores. Snow fell thick and blinding, and the wind whipped around the cabin, rattling the windows and whistling through cracks. Even with the fire in the stove, Laurie was cold. Now that it was light enough to see, she decided to dig through the trunk of clothes in the loft for extra layers.

She found a pair of thick wool socks with holes just beginning in the heels and a heavy sweater with a tear front and center. She brought these back down from the loft, tucking herself into the rocking chair with the quilt around her while she repaired them. The sweater went on over her own sweater, and she reveled in the warmth, though she had to roll the sleeves up to be able to use her hands. When the socks were darned, she slipped those on over her own socks. She might not quite be toasty, but she was warmer than she had been.

The snow lasted for two days. Laurie spent most of the time in the rocker pulled nearest the stove with all her layers and the quilt on top. She reread Pa's copy of *Tom Sawyer*, letting the too-long sleeves of the extra sweater cover her hands whenever she had to reach out of the quilt cocoon to turn the pages. She didn't bother trying to sleep upstairs while the storm lasted. Sometimes, when the wind blew particularly hard, she looked at the obscured window and worried for the men outside. Would they go out to feed the cattle in this? Would they get lost on the way and wander until they froze to death, all while less than one hundred yards from safety? Laurie had heard stories like that, and she had no desire to experience it in person.

When John finally shoveled the path to the cabin door and came inside, cheeks red and eyes watering from the wind, Laurie could have cried in relief. A part of her wanted to fling herself into his arms and hold him tight, to reassure herself that he was really safe and well. She'd have done it with Pa or Harvey. But while she'd come to consider John a friend, they certainly hadn't reached that level of familiarity.

She couldn't hide the relief in her voice, though, when she sighed, "You're safe."

He looked up from where he was dusting snow off his trousers. The smile on his face froze when he looked at her, and she wondered how peculiar she looked wearing multiple layers of sweaters. He blinked twice, then asked, "Were you worried?"

She nodded, though she blushed at the admission. "It was so cold."

"It wasn't so bad with all the animals around."

Laurie wondered if he was being completely truthful or if he just wanted to reassure her. But he was standing there, no worse for wear, so maybe it was the truth.

"What about you? Have you been alright the past few days?"

She nodded. "I had to borrow some clothes—" His throat bobbed as he glanced down at her sweaters again. "—and I might have used more coal than I should."

He nodded. "I plan for that. There's plenty of coal."

That didn't surprise her. He seemed to be good at preparing for whatever craziness the Wyoming winter threw at them. It was comforting to find herself unexpectedly in such capable hands. She'd spent months feeling uncertain and at a loss, left to her own devices after Pa's death. Self-reliance was exhausting when she trusted so few of her own decisions. She felt like she could breathe a little easier here, like John was someone she could depend on, despite her temporary situation.

It was a lovely, warm feeling but an unsettling one, and Laurie hugged her arms around herself. She had no business coming to rely on this man when she'd be leaving as soon as the snow melted.

"How deep is it?" She waved toward the door and the white powder piled outside.

"About two feet."

Her eyes widened. "You must have been shoveling all morning!"

He shrugged. "Most of it. We fed the cattle first thing, then Carlos handled the other chores while I started digging out the path. He knew I'd be too restless until…" His voice trailed off,

CHAPTER 12

and he looked down at his boots.

"Until what?" Laurie asked.

"Until I knew you were alright."

"Were you worried?" She echoed his own words back at him.

He rubbed the back of his neck. "A little. You could have fallen down the ladder from the loft or cut yourself or gone outside…"

His list of worries sounded a lot like the ones she'd wrestled with about *him*. "I'm perfectly fine." She took a step closer, wanting to reach out and lay a comforting hand on his arm but not coming quite near enough for that. "I stayed inside the whole time. I trust what you tell me—you haven't been wrong about the weather yet."

A soft smile crept onto his face. They looked at each other for a long minute. Laurie imagined him closing the distance between them and leaning just a little forward to press his lips to her forehead. But why would he do that, and why would she even think it? Even so, her skin tingled from the imaginary contact. He was just a concerned friend, and she was merely relieved that he was safe after the storm. That's all it was.

She blinked and looked down at her hands bunched in the ends of her overlong sleeves.

"Well, I'd better get back out there. Carlos will be wanting my help."

Laurie darted her gaze back to his. "Thank you for shoveling," she said. "I'll have dinner ready like usual."

As he left, she tried not to think about how comfortable she was becoming here, how much she liked the routine they'd built together over the past weeks. This was *his* home, not hers, and she'd be going back to Beth and Essie as soon as spring came.

***

She was wearing his sweater.

John had forgotten that some of his clothes had ended up in that trunk; he'd traded his sweater for George's last spring when his own had developed a hole that kept catching on everything. She'd mended the hole, he'd noticed. The garment was huge on her, and he'd seen hints of another, smaller sweater peeking out from underneath. The heavy layers failed to hide her shape, though. She looked as feminine and appealing as always, hugging herself in his sweater.

His sweater.

He didn't know why seeing her in something of his made his stomach swoop so wildly. But he liked it. Too much. He needed to rein himself in before she left and broke his heart.

Unless she didn't leave. He hadn't made much progress on a plan to woo her. Christmas had been the first step, the only concrete idea he'd had. He'd found that stone rose years ago, like he'd told her, and he'd tucked it away in the barn storage room, mostly forgotten. But every time he'd looked at it over the years, it had felt like it was waiting, just waiting for the right person. When he saw it again a few days before Christmas, he knew Laurie was that person. Even if she didn't stay, he wanted her to have that lasting token of his admiration.

"She doing alright?" Carlos's voice cut through John's musing as he put the shovel back in its place.

John nodded. She looked more than alright. She looked like the personification of all his dreams.

"Instead of pining in here, why don't you just talk to her?" Carlos gave John a light elbow to the ribs as he passed to get a saddle. "Get it all out in the open."

CHAPTER 12

"I can't—not yet. I don't know how she feels."

"From what I've heard, ladies like talking about their feelings."

"But what if she doesn't feel the same? Then everything will be awkward and miserable for the rest of the winter."

"Assuming she doesn't panic and take one of the horses and try to reach the train station through the snow."

John glared at him. "She wouldn't." Laurie had just told him that she trusted his word about the weather. She wouldn't try to find her way through all this snow. But he didn't like the suggestion that she could be so opposed to his affection that she'd run into danger.

Carlos only chuckled.

John decided to ignore his friend's needling. "The point is, I can't risk it. Her trust—her friendship—is too valuable. I won't ruin the time I have with her."

"Maybe you're right. But I hope you don't wait so long you lose her."

Carlos carried his saddle out of the storage room while John's stomach sank to his boots. He stood glowering at the doorway for a second until his friend called back to him.

"Head out of the clouds, *hombre*. There's still work to be done!"

While John completely failed to keep Laurie Kerstetter from his thoughts, he did manage to get the day's work done by the time the sun set and they both headed to the cabin to see what she had cooked that day. As usual, the house smelled incredible. John didn't know how she could use the same ingredients they did and make something so far beyond what they'd ever managed.

As they kicked off their boots, Carlos's eyes narrowed slightly on Laurie in John's sweater, the sleeves now rolled up so that she could stir something in a pot on the stove. He leaned close. "Yours?" he murmured.

John gave a single sharp nod, unable to take his eyes off her. He'd been surprised how young she was when she first arrived, and now he was struck by it again. Only a few years separated them, but she looked so small dwarfed by his sweater. She called out all his protective instincts, even as he knew that she was probably the most capable young woman he'd met.

John remembered his sister Missy's friends from Boston. None of them would have been caught dead cleaning stalls or milking cows. It was unlikely any of them could have cooked even one of the meals Laurie had; their families all hired others to do the heavy work. She impressed him with her skills, her work ethic, and her determination, not to mention her courage. The West needed women like Laurie Kerstetter. *He* needed her.

Finding a wife had been nowhere near his thoughts, not while he and George had been living the single life together, nor after George died and he had to keep the ranch going without his brother's help. But now he didn't know if he could bear going back to the way things had been before this amazing woman stumbled into his life.

Carlos nudged him, smirking, before crossing to the table and jovially congratulating Laurie on surviving another winter storm. John followed, warmed by the smile she sent him and the hope it lit within him. Could she come to care about him the way he already did about her? She'd been worried about him during the storm—that was a good sign, right? And how she'd gazed up at him and said she trusted him… He warmed all over just thinking about it. Yes, he'd let himself hope, and

CHAPTER 12

he'd keep trying to find ways to win her over.

Chapter 13

A few more weeks of their comfortable routine of chores and dinners and working side by side, and Laurie grew more and more unsettled over how much she liked it. How at peace she felt on the ranch. How easy it would be to start calling this place home. But she couldn't get attached, not to Andie and Cass, not to Moonbeam, who was fast becoming her favorite of the horses, and certainly not to the handsome rancher whose presence made her insides flutter. He was always polite, always kind, always gentle. He was still protective, but she could see he'd come to respect her abilities and trust her to do the work. But none of that meant that he wanted to make his home hers too. None of that meant he felt anything romantic toward her. And even if he did—even if she did toward him, which she still refused to admit—staying would be a risk. Mr. Knowles was waiting in Haven River Falls. He was probably furious that she'd slipped out of town just in time before the snow hit. Who knew what he'd do if she married someone else? It wouldn't be safe for her, or for John, if she stayed.

Even so, she couldn't deny that she enjoyed his company. She enjoyed their conversations about the animals and about her family farm. Even when they were working together in silence,

CHAPTER 13

she liked having him nearby. The time she spent alone in the cabin had come to feel emptier despite the chores that kept her busy. It was worse in the evening after the men had left for the barn and the lonely quiet closed in. All her life, she'd shared her home with someone, first Mama, Pa, and Harvey, then, for a few months, Beth, Essie, and baby Levi. Evenings had been a time to relax together, to chat comfortably about the day and plan for the morrow, to finish up little odds and ends, to read aloud in front of the fire. She missed that. It made her homesick for what used to be, for that sense of love and family, that sense of home. She hadn't truly felt it since she lost Pa; even her time in Harrisburg had felt like borrowing rather than belonging.

The homesickness clung to her like a wistful cloud as she did her chores in the morning. Andie nudged her shoulder with her nose and mooed mournfully, as though she knew Laurie was unhappy. Laurie smiled at the cow and gave her an extra pat.

Snow began to fall lightly as Laurie carried the eggs and milk back to the house. She'd found an old butter churn buried deep in storage as she was looking for something to fix the milking stool, which Cass had broken with an irritable kick. John had helped her fix the stool, and she'd brought the churn to the cabin and cleaned it. She'd make butter today to go with the roast and fresh bread. The sky was overcast, like her mood, but the fat flakes merely flurried down and caused no alarm.

Churning butter had never been Laurie's favorite task, but she appreciated it now. Every moment of busyness kept her mind away from how badly she wanted a home to belong to—if she admitted it, how much she wanted to belong to this one.

When John and Carlos came in for dinner, brushing snow off

their coats and tipping it from the brims of their hats, her mood brightened. It was such a familiar thing, men coming in from their work to food she'd prepared. They weren't her father and cousin, but she could pretend for a little while that she was back home before everything changed, that she'd found a place where she fit again.

Of course, that game of pretend couldn't last forever. Dinner ended, and the melancholy sank back over her like a shawl around her shoulders as the men moved to put their outdoor gear back on. She began to gather dishes and put them in the sink, unable to stifle a sigh.

***

Something had seemed off about Laurie tonight, John thought, and the feeling got stronger as he and Carlos prepared to leave. She seemed smaller, almost forlorn, and it broke his heart.

"I'm going to stay and help with the dishes," he murmured to his friend. Carlos could handle the last chores of the night; there wasn't much left to do. John needed to be here. Maybe Laurie would open up and tell him what was wrong.

She looked up, surprised, when he stepped beside her and began drying the dishes she washed. A small smile flitted across her face, there and gone. John missed her full grin, but he was grateful to have brought even such a tiny smile to her face. They worked in silence, comfortable together. John wanted to know the cause of her sadness, but he didn't want to talk and ruin the moment. Soon enough, though, the dishes were put away, the leftovers were covered and brought down to the root cellar to keep cool, and he had no further excuse to stay. But he didn't want to leave.

CHAPTER 13

Laurie stood leaning against the table, gazing absently at one night-black window. John stepped up beside her and put a hand on her arm. "What's wrong? You seem sad."

She shrugged, not answering, but her eyelids fluttered in a series of blinks that might mean she was fighting back tears.

"Talk to me," he whispered. "Let me help."

She lifted her eyes to his, and he ached for the tears swimming there. "I miss..." She swallowed, and his eyes followed the movement of her delicate throat before darting back up to her face. "I miss the way things used to be, before Pa died." A few tears leaked out then, and John couldn't help himself. He pulled her to him, wrapping his arms around her shoulders and letting her rest her head against his flannel shirt. She smelled like sweet cream and spices and fresh-baked bread, and he forced himself not to drag in a great big whiff.

"I wish I could turn back time for you," he murmured, wisps of her hair tickling his neck. "What can I do?"

She shook her head slightly against his shoulder, but he didn't want to accept that there was nothing he could do. He couldn't bear to see her suffer.

"How can I help you?" he asked again.

She sniffled for another minute, and he waited anxiously for her to say anything. Lifting her head, she stepped back, enough that he had to drop his arms but not so far that his hands couldn't find hers.

"Would you..." She bit her lip, and he fought to keep from pulling her close again. "Could you stay just a little longer? It's—it's so lonely here with no one to talk to in the evening."

John would have done just about anything she asked, and this aligned so perfectly with what he wanted himself. He led her to the rocking chairs, letting her pick her favorite as he added some coal to the stove. She pulled a quilt onto her lap—not the one from his bed, but another that he and George had brought with them. It was rather worse for wear, and he watched her take a needle and thread out of a small sewing kit. With tiny, neat stitches, she began to sew up one of the seams that had come loose. John watched her graceful fingers deftly take stitch after stitch.

"Why did you come west?" she asked after a moment.

"George was restless and seeking adventure." He still remembered his brother at twenty-five, standing from the breakfast table and announcing that he was fed up with the sameness of Boston and that he was going to buy himself a train ticket that morning. "I craved the kind of wide open spaces you can't come by in a city, so I decided to join him."

She nodded as though she understood his need for room to breathe. "How old were you?"

"Seventeen."

"And your parents didn't mind?"

John shrugged. "They weren't thrilled with the idea, but I think they were glad I was going along to keep George from doing anything too crazy. He'd been known to make decisions without taking enough time to think first."

"Are they still in Boston? Your family?"

"Yes. My parents, and my sister and another brother. Missy and Charles are both married by now and starting families."

"Have you been home to see them?"

John shook his head, a pang of guilt hitting him. "Not yet. I keep telling myself I will as soon as I have the ranch running smoothly enough that I can take a month off."

Laurie snorted. "I've lived among farmers all my life, and I've seen what winter looks like on your ranch. There's no such thing as a good time to leave for a month."

John grinned, as much at the cuteness of her snort as at her comment. "I guess I hoped I might hire more hands eventually and leave them in charge."

She nodded, holding her needle between pursed lips while she cut a new piece of thread for the next seam. Unable to tear his gaze from her mouth, John still jumped on the chance to turn the conversation toward her and the questions he'd been dying to have answers to.

"What about you? Why did you answer a bride advertisement?"

Laurie scrunched her nose and made a face. "Poor judgment," she muttered as she threaded the needle. "I know better than to listen to Essie, and yet somehow…"

Her fingers began their stitch work again, and John waited for her to say more.

"Pa died in March, and Harvey inherited the farm. He married his sweetheart in July, and I moved out to live with friends. I didn't have to—he didn't kick me out or anything, and Mary's a dear. But, I don't know… Without Pa, I just didn't want to stay. It was Harvey and Mary's home, not mine anymore." She fell silent for a minute. "The friends I stayed with, Essie and her older sister Beth, had been my neighbors for nearly all my life until they moved to Harrisburg. I was looking forward to being with them again, maybe making a life for myself there, but I hated the city. Essie and I found a page of mail-order bride ads, and we were looking at them just for a laugh. I saw the name Haven River Falls, and it stuck in my head until I wanted to see it. I responded to the ad, just to find out more, but the letters weren't… well, they weren't a lot of things. Essie was the one who suggested I come out and see the town and the man for myself. I could always turn around and come back, right?" She snorted again, this time in clear derision of how her choices worked out. Shaking her head, she muttered, "I even brought my mama's ring with me."

The thought of another man putting a ring on Laurie's finger made John's stomach knot with jealousy. But he couldn't say that, so he addressed her previous comment. "If you'd come at a different time of year, that plan would have worked." And then she would have made it to the train, and he'd never have met her. He couldn't regret the snow trapping her here on his ranch.

"Yes," she said. "But now there's a scorned cowboy who's issued unpleasant threats, and all I can hope is that the way to the train station clears before the pass into town." She choked up then, fear and pain mingling in a scowl.

John's own glower was fiercer. "He *threatened* you?"

The words came out as a growl. Laurie nodded, not meeting his eyes. Whatever Knowles had said still upset her deeply. John almost wished he could cross the pass just so that he could find the man and deck him. The cowboy was a rogue; John had employed him one spring for branding and never again. He took a slow breath and leaned forward in his chair, resting his elbows on his knees, angling to get into Laurie's line of sight.

"You're safe here," he said, gentling his voice but unable to completely erase the growl. "I promised you that when you arrived. I won't let him hurt you."

Her sweet-caramel eyes lifted to his. "Thank you."

The poor girl looked like she could use a change of subject. "Tell me more about your friend Essie. She sounds like fun, if not the best advisor."

CHAPTER 13

This did the trick: her expression lightened, and she told him about her friends, and when prompted, about her cousin.

"He's more like a brother, really," she said, shifting the quilt on her lap so that she could reach another frayed seam. "His pa and mine were brothers, and his died in the war. His mama passed a few years later, and he came to live with us. I was barely more than a baby then, so we were raised together nearly all my life." She glanced over at John and smiled. "He'd like you."

Her words sent warmth rushing through him, though she probably didn't mean them the way he wanted her to. He wanted her brother-like cousin to approve him as her future husband. She probably only meant that as a farmer and a rancher, they'd get along.

They fell silent, but it was the comfortable quiet he'd grown to love with her. He had no idea how long the silence stretched, and he'd long since lost track of what time it was. The sun had already gone down when they'd come in for dinner, and he couldn't guess how long they'd been talking. Hours, maybe. He should excuse himself back out to the barn. He'd already been alone with her longer than he should have.

When he looked over, his mouth open to say the words, he saw Laurie's head resting back against the chair, lolling slightly to the side as she slept. Her fingers had loosened their grip on the needle, and he took it from her lap before it fell to the floor to be found by her foot in the morning.

"Laurie?" He rested his hand on hers, but she only smiled in her sleep and sighed. He shook her shoulder gently but got no more response. She was out.

John grinned. Laurie Kerstetter looked more adorable than ever with her long lashes brushing her freckled pink cheeks.

He still couldn't guess how she might feel about a potential relationship with him, but he loved that she was relaxed enough in his presence to fall asleep so soundly.

Carefully, he removed the quilt from her lap and scooped her into his arms. She sighed and snuggled into his shoulder, and his heart swelled. Carrying her up the ladder to the loft was no easy feat—light as she was, it was an awkward climb—but he soon had her tucked in for the night. He brushed a wisp of hair from her forehead and sat back on his heels for one last look. A thrill shot through him, and he fled down the ladder, but nothing could make him forget the sight of the sleeping woman of his dreams—in his bed.

John crossed to the door in three quick strides, slamming his feet into his boots and throwing his arms into his coat, needing to get away before he lost any more of his heart to a woman who may never love him back and who had every intention of leaving. He unlatched the door and jumped back as the wind ripped it from his hand and blew it back against the wall, freezing snow and sleet pounding the mat on the floor. John forced the door shut again, panting. He had been so caught up in talking to Laurie that he hadn't noticed the changing weather. He couldn't go out in this. Even the short walk to the barn would be treacherous and potentially deadly. He'd be soaked through in seconds, and he shouldn't risk slipping and injuring something. It was safer to shelter here in the cabin.

He sighed and pulled off all the outerwear he'd just put on. He added more coal to the stove, blew out the candles, then sat back in the rocking chair he'd vacated only a few minutes before, stretching his legs out long and pulling the half-mended quilt over him. He smiled as he rested his head back against the wood of the chair. The night hadn't ended as he'd expected, but

CHAPTER 13

every moment with Laurie Kerstetter was worth treasuring.

***

The gray beyond the single loft window was already lightening toward dawn when Laurie woke. She rubbed her eyes, disoriented. She didn't remember getting ready for bed. Sitting up, she realized that she was still wearing her dress and sweaters—she *hadn't* gotten ready for bed. She must have dozed off in the rocking chair. Her stomach gave a happy little flutter at the idea of John carrying her up to bed. She should be appalled: falling asleep with a man in the room was entirely improper. And yet, she couldn't work up the requisite horror. She'd liked how his arms felt around her when she'd broken down last evening, liked feeling cared for and valued, and she only wished she could have been awake to remember those strong arms carrying her upstairs.

Laurie stumbled down the ladder in the dark. She'd forgotten to bring up a candle and flint enough times that she could find her way through the cabin by feel. She could see where the paler rectangles of the windows were, but there wasn't enough light yet to illuminate anything inside.

The first step was to find one of the candles that she'd left on the table. She'd light it at the stove when she added coal. Shuffling in her socks across the wood floor, her outstretched hands found the table easily enough, and within seconds she had a candlestick in her grasp. Navigating to the stove was trickier, but she'd done it before. Her free hand found the back of the chair she'd sat in last night, and she skirted it, knowing she should have a straight shot to the stove, and she'd need to be careful if she didn't want to burn herself on it.

Suddenly, her foot met with an unexpected obstacle, and she tripped, her feet tangling in thick fabric. She fell forward with an alarmed squeak, landing half across the second rocking chair. Except what she was sprawled across didn't feel like the wood of the chair seat, and rocking chairs shouldn't grunt in surprise. She struggled to regain her feet.

"Hey, it's alright, it's just me." Big hands found her arms, and she stilled. Her panic calmed at his sleep-roughened voice.

"John? What are you doing here?"

"The weather got bad last night, so it wasn't safe to go out. Sorry. Didn't mean to scare you."

She shook her head. "It's fine. I just..." She trailed off, struggling to find a coherent thought in the blankness of her mind. She really should get off his lap. With a gasp, she tried to push herself upright.

"Hang on, there." John's hands found her waist, and he steadied her as she righted herself and untangled her feet from the folds of the quilt. "You good?"

"Yes, thanks." Her voice came out breathy and shaken. Well, of course it did, this wasn't how her mornings usually started.

"Stay right where you are. I'll light the candle."

Laurie realized then that she'd dropped the candlestick in the confusion. She felt the movement of air in the dark as John lifted aside the quilt and stood up, then the dim red glow from the embers as he opened the stove door and lit the candle. He handed it back to her before adding coal and shutting the door again. He straightened and turned to her. They were standing too close together, but Laurie's feet were nailed to the floor. She could do nothing but look up into those blue-green eyes that glinted in the flickering candlelight. He ran a hand through his hair, longer now than when she'd first seen him.

CHAPTER 13

It curled a little around his ears. His beard was longer and thicker now too, and she marveled at how it made him look strong and ruggedly appealing, while Mr. Knowles's whiskers had only looked unkempt and disgusting.

John glanced toward the door. "We should wait until there's more light before we try making our way to the barn. The path's probably sheer ice."

Laurie blinked and nodded. She'd forgotten all about morning chores. "Breakfast first," she said. "Pancakes and fried eggs sound good?"

He chuckled, the deep, warm sound washing over her. "We usually make do with coffee or porridge at most."

She frowned. "I could bring you food in the morning."

"No, ma'am," he said. "You do enough, and we appreciate every bit." He grinned then. "But I wouldn't say no to pancakes and eggs today."

Laurie used her candle to light the others and set about mixing batter. She cracked the last of yesterday's eggs into an oiled frying pan, and within a few minutes, she and John were sitting at the table with plates of breakfast. Since it was just the two of them, they sat side by side on the bench. Laurie expected to feel awkward and shy around him, given the way he'd carried her to bed last night and she'd woken him up this morning. But they chatted as easily as if sharing breakfast and getting ready together to go out to do chores were not an unprecedented thing.

The melancholy that had dragged at Laurie yesterday was nowhere to be found. It had been replaced by a different longing. The past had lost its stranglehold on her sometime during the evening and morning she'd spent with John. Now she found herself dreaming of a future where every day ended with the two of them sitting by the fire and each new day began with sharing breakfast. She refused to examine the wish too closely. It was a futile dream, anyway. The specter of Mr. Knowles still lurked, ready to become a real threat as soon as the snow melted. Even so, the wish lingered, refusing to be extinguished. John had said he'd protect her, that she'd always be safe here. Could she trust him in that too? Could she stop fearing a low-down cowboy and make a life for herself on this ranch she wanted so badly to call home?

Chapter 14

More snow fell a week later, dumping a fresh four inches overnight. It was heavy, wet snow, and Laurie was glad there wasn't much of it as she waded through it to the barn. Snow like that would be awfully heavy to shovel.

But it was perfect for snowballs.

She bent down just outside the barn door to scoop up a handful, pressing it into a ball as she'd done countless times with Harvey and with the other students after school on snowy days. She carried it behind her back as she entered the barn. As she'd come to expect, John looked up from where he stood by the stove when the door creaked open. His face lit up in the smile she loved before his ears reddened and he turned away, back to the coffee he was pouring into his tin cup. As soon as his back was half turned, Laurie let loose the snowball, unable to hold back her cackle as the wet projectile exploded against John's shoulder, spraying his face and neck with cold snow.

He gasped, his shoulders shooting upward as snow got into his collar, and he rounded on her, barely remembering to set his cup down before chasing after her. Laurie shrieked and sprinted back outside, scooping up more snow and balling it between her hands as she put distance between herself and her pursuer. She turned and lobbed it at John as he packed a ball of his own. Soon, white missiles flew through the air as fast as they could make and throw them. Laurie was a pretty good shot, but she hadn't reckoned with the fact that John had spent years roping cattle. He had a strong arm and remarkable aim, and he definitely got more hits on her than she did. But Laurie was wearing two coats and a sweater underneath, so she barely felt a thing.

Carlos watched from the barn door, chuckling. "Alright, *niños*," he said. "Enough playing. There's work to be done."

Laurie, breathless from trying to dodge snowballs, called, "What are *niños*?"

"Children," Carlos called over his shoulder as he reentered the barn.

Giggling, Laurie couldn't deny that that's what they'd been acting like, but she couldn't regret it. She grinned at John as they both moved toward the barn. He dusted off his hands, eyes widening as she bent to make one more snowball. At this range, she couldn't have missed him, and he knew it.

His eyes narrowed, though they twinkled with fun. "I'll throw you in a snowdrift," he warned.

Laurie shook her head and put a finger to her lips, then pointed at the barn where Carlos had disappeared. He smirked and opened the door so she could enter first.

Carlos was walking toward the farthest stall with tack for Crescent. "About time," he teased without looking back.

Laurie wound up and let the snowball fly. It hit Carlos right between the shoulder blades and exploded in a mess of wet white powder.

John snickered, and the sound set Laurie off. Soon they were both laughing uncontrollably, and even Carlos joined in. In a minute, they pulled themselves together and got to work, but the lightheartedness remained.

***

The first of the early calves was born in late February. John found mother and baby nestled in the lee of the windbreak he'd built in the middle of the pasture, the mama still licking the calf clean of the steaming afterbirth. John hurried back to the barn for a blanket. He found Laurie halfway through filling the horses' stalls with clean hay, and he stopped just long enough to ask her to pile bedding in one of the spare stalls too.

She straightened, pushing hair out of her eyes with one coat sleeve. "Is there a baby coming?"

"Already here," he said over his shoulder as he strode toward the door. "Didn't expect her to go yet."

He left the barn before she could respond, riding back out to the mama as quickly as the snowy fields allowed. He hollered to Carlos, who was checking the rest of the herd, and the cowboy turned to follow along. Carlos used the rope that hung from his saddle to loop the mother's neck and restrain her just long enough for John to wrap the blanket around the newborn and drape him over the saddle. Once he was in the saddle behind the calf and moving back toward the barn, Carlos released the unhappy mother. She followed John to the barn, lowing all the way.

Inside, the stall door was open and hay was mounded to make a comfortable bed for the two. John lifted the calf down and laid him in the stall, where moments later he was reunited with his mother. John closed the stall door and leaned on the top for a moment, watching the pair. Laurie came up beside him to peer over the stall door with him.

"Ever seen a newborn calf?"

She shook her head. "I didn't realize they were so... gangly." She giggled. "He's all legs."

John chuckled. He loved her laugh, and he was glad he got to share a moment like this with her. Maybe enough of these moments of wonder would make her fall in love with the ranch. Maybe enough moments of laughter could make her fall in love with *him*.

There were two other expecting mothers in the herd. John had thought they'd all be due late in March or April, but the surprise appearance of the first calf made him more concerned about the others. He and Carlos moved the other mothers to the smaller horse paddock where they could check on them frequently. He hoped spring would come before either mother was ready to give birth, and judging by the surprise calf already in the barn, an early snowmelt would be preferable.

Hoping for the snow to melt early sat wrong with John. That would cut down his time with Laurie. Their evening together played on repeat through his mind, with emphasis on the moments of contact: hugging her while she cried, carrying her up to the loft, catching her when she tripped over his quilt-covered feet in the morning. He wished for more such moments, but no opportunities had presented since then. He often stayed a few extra minutes to help her wash up after dinner, and twice he'd stayed to sit and chat in the rockers a little longer. But he couldn't leave Carlos to do all the evening chores too often, and he didn't want to overstep with his guest. Just because he came alive in her company didn't mean she felt the same.

Their conversations had undergone a shift since that stormy

night, however, and his heart desperately hoped that it meant something. They still had plenty of comfortable silences while they worked together, but they also talked about deeper, more important things. Laurie told him more about her friends and family, about the goats she'd raised and how she'd been running her father's house since her mother had died when she was thirteen. It was no wonder she was so capable, but he wished her skills hadn't come at such a cost. She told him about the books she'd brought with her, her mother's favorite and her father's, and how she'd reread them both several times during the storms and the quiet evenings.

John told her more about George and about how things were when they'd first started ranching. Neither of them had known anything about cattle, but they'd both loved the land. Of course, now John could see that they'd been doing well, but he couldn't call it thriving. Not now that he knew how much better it could be with a good woman by his side. He kept this last reflection from Laurie, though. There was still too much of winter left to risk ruining everything.

He told her about Missy and Charles back in Boston and what it had been like growing up with three siblings. She said she'd never felt like an only child, not with Harvey around, but she admitted to sometimes wishing there had been more of them.

Somehow, every conversation with Laurie had come to be meaningful, no matter the subject.

A couple of weeks later, they moved the mother and calf—Polaris and baby Orion; she'd named them in honor of George's tradition, with a soft smile that melted John's heart—into a clean stall so that they could clear out the old one. Laurie, he'd noticed, took every opportunity she could get to gaze at the calf, stopping any time she passed their stall.

"I used to think," she said, pitching fresh hay into the cleaned stall, "that goat kids were the cutest thing. They're tiny and adorable, and I couldn't help cuddling them every chance I got. But I don't know—Orion may be cuter. I mean, those *eyes*." She clasped her hands under her chin and widened her own eyes, batting the lashes as if she were imitating the calf.

John chuckled, taking the cows' water bucket to fill with snow to melt by the stove. "They are impressive," he agreed, while secretly wanting to tell her that her coffee-and-sweet-cream eyes put Orion's to shame, without any effort at all.

"But even Orion can't compete with Levi," she added, giving the cows one last glance before leaving the stall and leaning the pitchfork against the wall. She came to stand by the stove with him, warming her hands in their gloves. "When that baby smiles, I swear the angels sing." She grinned.

John had a sudden vision of Laurie with a dimple-cheeked baby in her arms and a toddler clutching her skirts, both with the same warm brown hair and eyes as hers. Or maybe lighter blue-green eyes? He was struck breathless with the longing for those babies to be his.

"Laurie," he murmured, his mouth preparing to spill his heart's confession without any input from his mind.

She looked up at him, her perfect pink lips smiling and sweet. If he just leaned down a little… Not until he told her his truth. If she responded well, he'd kiss her silly.

But before he could say another word, Carlos burst into the barn.

"Got a broken fence along the north side of the pasture," he said, stalking into the supply room for tools. "No runaways yet, but once they find it…"

CHAPTER 14

No need to say more. "I'll saddle Star and be right behind you." The last thing they needed was to be rounding up lost cattle in the cold and snow when they couldn't ride to town for extra hands.

He glanced back at Laurie, the moment lost. "This is almost melted," she said, gesturing to the bucket of snow. "I'll take care of it. You go."

He tipped his hat to her and went to get a saddle.

***

The snow began to melt in early April. Laurie noticed the shrinking dirty white piles with dismay. The air had lost its bite, warming enough that she could leave her extra shearling layer in the cabin and just wear her wool coat when she went outside. It wouldn't be long before the track to Table Rock station would be cleared of its obscuring white blanket. She could get to the train soon. She could go back to Beth and Essie.

Go *back*, not go *home*. The weight of her impending departure sat heavily on her. Despite her efforts to keep emotional distance, she'd grown attached to Orion and the newest little calf, Ursa. She was running out of astronomical names, so maybe she was leaving just in time. But it felt wrong. It felt like she'd be leaving her heart behind on the ranch. Because more than caring about the animals, she'd become irreversibly attached to the man who owned them. John was more than handsome; he was kind, generous, and thoughtful. He was courageous, strong, and a hard worker. He listened to her, respected her, made her feel valued. But was that all? Was that enough?

Another snowstorm hit, thick heavy flakes settling over the patches of brown earth that had begun to emerge. Laurie could have danced as she watched out the window. This snow would keep her here just a little longer.

One morning, she left the barn with the milk and eggs at the same time John led Crescent out, saddled and ready to go check the herd. He paused before getting into the saddle and looked north, away from the ranch buildings and across the wide prairie that was spotted brown and white like one of the native ponies she'd seen drawings of. Laurie paused too. She loved the view, but she also wanted to savor every brief moment she had with him.

"Still not safe to ride to Table Rock," he said. "Not for another day or two, depending on the weather."

Laurie nodded. "Alright." Maybe by then she could find another reason to delay. The threat of Mr. Knowles—less frightening now after months away from him—felt less urgent than the pain of leaving.

John glanced quickly at her. She caught a flash of something in his expression—longing, maybe? Was he as reluctant for her to leave as she was?

She tried to think of something to say to prolong the conversation. "Will you be back in time for lunch? I'm thinking of biscuits with gravy and baked corn."

He smiled. "I'll make sure I'm back. I've got work to do in the greenhouse this afternoon anyway."

"Greenhouse?" Laurie asked, turning to study the farm buildings. "I haven't seen the greenhouse. Where is it?"

"Behind the cabin. I'll show you if you like."

"I'd love to see it." Laurie watched his smile grow, adding a sparkle to his blue-green eyes. "I love gardening. We never had a greenhouse, though."

"Growing season's too short without one," he said. "I just need to make sure everything's in good repair. We have some seeds saved from last year, but I need to see what more we'll need to pick up in town." He swung up into the saddle and tipped his hat. "Until lunch."

Laurie watched him ride away until he was out of sight then went inside to start cooking.

***

After lunch, John stayed to help Laurie clean up, then they walked together around to the back of the cabin. The snow had been melting steadily after the last storm, leaving the ground covered in muddy slush. Laurie held her skirt up with one hand, her other resting on his arm for balance as she picked her way through the mess. John didn't mind at all. He basked in her closeness, wondering for the hundredth time if today was the day he should speak up. He'd come close that day in the barn, but after he'd gone with Carlos to mend the fence, his rational mind had retaken control and reminded him that it was still too soon, there were still weeks before she could leave. So he hadn't tried to revisit the aborted conversation. But he couldn't put it off forever. Even his declaration that it wasn't safe to ride to Table Rock was stretching the truth. Maybe it wasn't advisable with the snow still half covering the ground, but someone who knew the way could find it.

He felt a twinge of guilt at the half-truth. Laurie had come to trust his judgment, and he was taking advantage of that faith.

But with her beside him, leaning on his arm as they squished through the slush and mud, he couldn't think beyond keeping her here a little longer, extending her stay by just a few more days. If she turned him down and wanted to leave, he'd at least have these last few memories.

As they rounded the corner of the house, the greenhouse came into view. It looked nothing like the sleek steel-and-glass buildings that had become popular among Boston elites before John had left the city, but it had the same effect. It was a simple lean-to built against the back of the house. He'd built the frame of old wood reclaimed from one of the buildings they'd torn down when they'd bought the land. He'd fitted in window glass salvaged wherever he could find it. The effect was odd and eclectic, but it was sturdy and functional.

John checked the door as he opened it for her. The latch was still secure, and the frame hadn't settled too much over the winter. Inside, there were long, narrow garden beds running on either side of a central walkway. Trellises lined the wall shared by the house so that they could grow beans and peas both before and after the season permitted. He'd tried training squash to grow upright too, rather than sprawling, with limited success. On the side opposite the house, he'd built a shelf at about chest height, just where the angled wood-and-glass roof met the wall. In previous years, they'd used it for starter pots, herbs, and storing tools, while the garden bed below was usually occupied by shorter plants, like tomatoes, potatoes, carrots, and lettuce. He'd moved all the tools and pots to the barn for storage over the winter, in case the snow got too heavy on the roof and broke through the glass. No sense in having to replace everything rather than just a window. As he looked around, however, John was pleased. The greenhouse was overall in good shape, with a few warped boards and gaps that he could fix easily. He turned to Laurie, who was smiling

CHAPTER 14

broadly.

"This is wonderful," she said when she noticed him watching her. "It's so much warmer in here, and I can just imagine this space full of growth and life."

John fell for her just a little harder. Could this woman be any more perfect for this ranch? For him? He lifted his hat from his head, running his other hand through his hair before he replaced it. He should just ask her now.

"Do you think... Would you..." All the words he'd rehearsed over the last months got lost on the way to his mouth as he was distracted by her wide, brown-sugar-sweet eyes looking up at him expectantly. He closed the distance between them without being aware that he'd moved, drawn by her magnetic pull. He stuffed his hands into his pockets to keep from reaching out for her as he struggled to form a coherent sentence.

"Thought I'd find you here," Carlos's voice said from behind him, accompanied by the door's creak.

Laurie took a startled step back, and John closed his eyes, groaning internally. How had his friend managed to interrupt them *again*? He turned slowly. Carlos had his arms full of gardening tools and a glass jar filled with paper packets of seeds.

"Sorry for interrupting," the cowboy said. His expression was chagrinned, though his dark eyes twinkled. "Here's most of the stuff from the storage room. Figured I'd save you a trip since I was heading this way anyway. I was just checking the expectant mamas, and there might be a problem with one of 'em."

John sighed. Another potentially perfect moment lost. "Let's go." He half turned to face Laurie. "Sorry. Maybe you could look through the seeds and think about what ought to go where? And what else we'll need?"

She nodded and accepted the jar from Carlos, who set the tools on the shelf.

John followed his friend out of the greenhouse, waiting until they were out of earshot before muttering, "I thought you *wanted* me to talk to her."

"I do."

"Fine way to show it. That's the second time you've interrupted."

"Sorry, *hombre*." Carlos's ever-cheerful disposition was unmoved by John's grouching, which was both irritating and comfortingly familiar. "But one of the mothers doesn't look like she's carrying quite right, and she's not showing interest in food."

By the time they were done with the expectant cows, dusk was falling and it was time to feed the herd and start chores. John tried to keep his mind on his tasks and not in the greenhouse with Laurie, but his success was limited.

"Another two weeks and we can release the herd onto the range," Carlos said as they finished.

John nodded. "We'll need to hire a few hands—two or three should do it."

"I'll go to town tomorrow. Make a list for the mercantile."

"Think the pass is open?"

Carlos shrugged. "Open enough."

John felt a lump of ice sink into his belly. The barrier that had protected Laurie from that wretched Knowles was gone. Their time was up—he'd have to either take her to the train station or to the preacher. He'd promised he'd protect her, and he meant it.

CHAPTER 14

✲✲✲

Laurie was disappointed when John didn't return to the greenhouse that afternoon. She wanted to hear whatever he'd been about to say. There had been an intensity in his gaze that made her heart race, and she had a hard time concentrating on gardening. She finally gave up and went inside, bringing the jar of seed packets with her. She dug through her carpetbag for paper and pen, then sat and made lists as dinner cooked. She listed the seeds they had and also what she would buy if this were her old garden back at the farm. Her mind wandered, picturing the greenhouse bursting with life, imagining herself picking and preserving vegetables for the next winter. But she wouldn't be here that long, she reminded herself. Whatever she helped plant, John and Carlos would have to harvest alone.

She sighed, wistfully wondering what John had been meaning to tell her earlier. Her heart said it was important.

As soon as the men came in for dinner, John apologized. "I never meant to leave you alone out there," he said. "But it was one thing after another."

"I understand."

She smiled so he'd know she wasn't mad, but his answering smile wasn't as bright as usual, and there was a faint furrow between his brows. He crossed the room to her side, obviously preoccupied by something upsetting.

"What is it?" she asked softly.

"The pass into town might be open already." He frowned at the soup pot bubbling on the stove. "Carlos is going to check tomorrow."

Ice flooded Laurie's veins. "Oh," was all she managed.

John nodded. They stood in silence for a long moment, while

Carlos sliced the loaf of bread at the table and ignored them.

"If the pass is clear, he'll go to the mercantile to restock," John added, as if just now remembering the practical details. "Would you mind helping us make a list of what's needed?"

"Of course."

They sat down to eat. When they were finished, Laurie tore the paper she'd been using earlier in half, copying over the list of seeds needed and adding a list of ingredients that they'd run low on or were out of completely. John and Carlos rattled off things that they'd need for the animals or to repair tools and tack that had broken during the winter, and she wrote those down as well. Finally, their suggestions petered out, and Laurie handed the list to Carlos.

"Will you be leaving first thing?"

"Yes, ma'am."

"Would you be kind enough to call on Martha Brown to let her know I'm safe? I feel awful that she's probably been worried about me all this time."

Carlos assured her that he would, getting to his feet and moving toward the door. John followed, pausing a moment to rest a hand on Laurie's shoulder.

"I wish I could stay longer," he said, that same intensity deepening his blue-green eyes, "but I've got to help get things ready for the morning. Will you—will you go riding with me tomorrow? I figure you haven't gotten to see much since you've been here. Maybe a picnic?"

Laurie beamed. "That sounds perfect." A whole day with him would more than make up for the afternoon they'd missed in the greenhouse.

He smiled and leaned in to brush a kiss on her temple. Her breath caught and heat radiated from the place his lips touched.

CHAPTER 14

Before she could say or do anything, he was gone.

Chapter 15

Carlos left at first light. Laurie stepped out of the cabin just as he was mounting Milky Way in the yard. Two of the other horses followed at the end of lead lines, ready to serve as pack horses on the way back from town.

"Horses will have better luck in the pass than a wagon if it's not totally thawed yet," John said, watching the cowboy and the three horses head toward the track that would lead them south to town. "And if it's still closed, he'll turn around and come back."

Laurie nodded. Yesterday she would have hoped the pass would still be closed. Today she was going riding with John, and she'd find a time to ask him... everything. About last night's kiss. About what he'd been saying before they were interrupted in the greenhouse. How he felt. She didn't know how to bring up the subject without sounding forward, but she needed to know. If he saw her as no more than a friend, she'd pack her bag and take the train as soon as it was safe to do so. But that kiss had to mean something, didn't it? They'd been friends for a few months now, and that was the first time he'd done anything like *that*.

They did their chores in the barn in the peaceful quiet that Laurie had grown to love. Then, while John saddled the horses,

CHAPTER 15

Laurie took the eggs and milk back to the house and grabbed the bundle of food she'd wrapped in a towel. It was all simple food that was easy to carry and eat outside—bread and butter left from last night, some of the last carrots and apples from the root cellar, dried beef strips. Nothing fancy, but she was excited nonetheless. Maybe someday, if their conversations today went the way she hoped, she'd purchase a real picnic basket and they could take a proper picnic with pie and potato salad and cold chicken. She smiled as she carried the bundle back outside.

Moonbeam carried an empty saddlebag, and Laurie stowed her bundle inside. Crescent carried a rifle within easy reach. Laurie stared at it. It wasn't that she'd never seen a gun—Pa and Harvey were both accomplished hunters, and she remembered Mr. Brown's pistol—but she'd never seen one around the ranch.

"You never know what you'll meet out there, especially after a long winter," John said, seeing where she was looking. "It's still wild country, after all. We always carry a weapon when we ride out."

Now that she thought about it, Laurie remembered a long shape slung behind Carlos's saddle that morning, though it had been too dark to see it for what it was.

"Of course," she said, blinking and looking up at him. "I guess I just never noticed before."

"Can you shoot?"

Laurie nodded. "Well enough." She wouldn't like to rely on her own hunting to survive, but Pa had taught both her and Harvey how to handle a gun.

"Good. It's a necessary skill out here."

Did he think she'd be staying long enough to need that skill?

Did he want her to? But she couldn't think why else he'd say something like that. If they met anything dangerous today, *he* was the one with the gun.

He helped her into the saddle, his hands on her waist to give her a boost since she was so short and there was no mounting block. She wondered for a second how Carlos managed, since they were about the same height, and wondered too if she might ever learn to swing into the saddle from the ground on her own. Did she even want to learn, if the alternative was having John's strong hands supporting her? She grinned down at him once she was settled, and he grinned back before swinging himself effortlessly onto Crescent.

He led them north and west, away from the farm buildings and the way to town. Laurie marveled at the broad, flat countryside much as she had when she'd been carried from the train station in Mr. Harrison's wagon. The yard and the pastures nearest the house were a sea of mud from the melting snow and churning hooves, but out here the remains of last year's brown grasses were showing the barest hints of new green, while the only remaining patches of snow were in the few shaded hollows. While she missed the rolling hills of central Pennsylvania, Laurie reveled in the wide expanse of sky stretching as far as she could see. She only wished that gray clouds didn't obscure so much of the gorgeous blue. She was glad of her coat because the breeze was sharp and the sun only peeked out occasionally from behind the clouds.

They rode slowly, taking their time. John alternated between studying the land around them and looking at Laurie. As they rode, he told her what he'd learned about the plants they were seeing, about the prairie dogs that popped out of their holes in the distance, about the hawks that swooped overhead.

CHAPTER 15

"You've learned a lot in seven years. Did you know any of this before you left Boston?"

"None," he said. "And there's so much I still don't know. I reckon the land will keep teaching me until the day I die."

Laurie liked that image of rancher and ranch working together for long, harmonious years.

Around noon they reached a small hollow with a handful of trees. One had fallen, and the trunk made a perfect bench. They ground tied the horses, and Laurie got out the food she'd packed.

"It's not much," she said, laying it out on the trunk between them. "I wasn't sure how to transport a fancier picnic."

"And I didn't give you much time to plan or cook." John smiled at her. "It's not the food that matters so much as the company."

Laurie blushed. Did he realize how comments like that made her heart race? Did he mean anything by them? It was time to get answers.

"What were you starting to say yesterday in the greenhouse?" she ventured. "We never got a chance to finish the conversation."

John took a bite of buttered bread and chewed it slowly. He watched the horses graze on the mix of brown and green grass.

"You seem to like the ranch well enough," he said eventually.

"I do." Laurie didn't quite dare admit that she loved the place already.

"And you don't mind the chores?"

"Not at all."

"The work only gets harder in the summer," he commented. "Winter is our slow time."

"I know," she said, trying to read his expression, but his hat shadowed his face. She was used to summers of hard work—deep cleaning the house, growing and preserving produce for the winter—and she doubted the work would be much different here.

She waited for him to get to his point. This was all leading up to something, and she desperately wanted to hear it. She held her breath as he said, "I know it's not what you planned, but—"

Laurie interrupted him with a shriek as big, cold raindrops splashed onto her head. She scrambled to gather the food back into the towel she'd wrapped it in. No sooner had she stowed it in the saddlebag than John was tossing her into the saddle as if she weighed no more than a bag of flour. Laurie could see now that, while she'd been distracted talking to John, the clouds had been gathering to block more and more of the blue sky until they let loose. She shivered. She'd left her hat and scarf at the cabin, not thinking she'd need them in the warmer April air. Now water ran into the collar of her coat and trailed down her spine, chilling her. John handed her Moonbeam's reins and mounted himself, but before he urged the horses along, he swept his hat off his head and plunked it onto Laurie's. She gasped in surprise. His hair was soon plastered wetly to his head, falling in his eyes and revealing how long it had grown over the winter. Meanwhile, the Stetson was still warm from his heat, and it stopped the rain from running down inside Laurie's coat. Laurie felt warmth flare inside her from the sweetness of his action. He truly cared about her wellbeing.

These thoughts occupied her as they cantered back to the cabin, quickly retracing the steps they'd spent the whole morning making. There was no opportunity to talk—the pounding of rain and hooves were too loud. At last they slowed

CHAPTER 15

to a walk, taking time for the horses to cool down and more carefully find their footing as they approached the muddy yard.

They dismounted in front of the cabin. "You go in and change into dry things," John said, coming to take Moonbeam's head. "I'll take care of the horses."

"I can help." Laurie knew that the horses would need all that mud washed off their legs and bellies.

John shook his head, droplets of water flinging from his long, sopping hair. "I can't let you catch cold."

"You don't have to coddle me." Laurie scowled. "I'm not fragile."

John laughed. "Don't I know it. But you are precious. Let me do this, Laurie."

His words disarmed her completely, and she nodded. But before she left him, she plucked his hat from her own head and set it on his. "Thank you," she murmured.

She slipped into the cabin as he led the horses across the yard to the barn.

***

Laurie was hoping that John would come to the cabin before Carlos got back. They only needed a few more uninterrupted minutes to finish the conversation, she was sure. But there was no sign of him as she hung her wet clothes over the rocking chairs by the stove and cooked dinner.

Both men looked a bit bedraggled when they tromped into the house at sunset. Their hair looked mussed and damp from being toweled dry. Laurie liked the way John's curled over his forehead and at the back of his neck. She wanted to tease him about it and tug on those curls, but his hair wouldn't have gotten wet at all if he hadn't given her his hat, and she was grateful.

She dished out bowls of onion soup to warm them up before carving the chicken she'd had roasting in the dutch oven all day.

"Was the pass open, then?" she asked after a minute filled with only the sound of slurping soup.

"Yes, ma'am," Carlos said. "The path's a mess, but we made it there and back."

"And got caught in the rain, too," Laurie said.

Carlos nodded with a wry smile to match her own.

"We unloaded everything in the barn," John said. "We'll move the foodstuffs to the cabin when the rain clears."

"Did you see Martha?"

Carlos nodded, a faint pink tinging his olive cheeks. "Happened to meet her and her ma in the mercantile. Seems Wes Harrison has made a trip out to Table Rock already to order new stock and pick up the mail. Speaking of…" He pulled a small parcel of envelopes from his back pocket. "You had some letters waiting for you."

Laurie saw Essie's writing on two of the envelopes and Harvey's on two others. Her heart clenched. She was almost afraid to read what Harvey had written.

"From your cousin?" John asked.

Laurie nodded, the letters clutched tightly in her hand. "He's probably threatening to come hunt me down if I don't write back." She said it as if it were a joke, but she doubted she was far off. Time to get back on the subject. She asked Carlos, "Did you tell them that I was safe?"

"I did, and they were right glad to hear it. Miss Brown burst into tears on the spot, and her ma hugged me for bringing

CHAPTER 15

the news." The pink in his cheeks darkened, and his eyes got distant for a minute. Then he frowned and looked back at Laurie. "I may have made a mess of things, though."

Laurie frowned in confusion. "How so?"

"Well, Mrs. Harrison was there at the counter when I told the Browns where you'd sheltered for the winter. I reckon she looked a mite scandalized at the thought of a young lady staying the winter with a couple of bachelors."

Laurie's heart sank. It had been a choice between staying at Newcomb Ranch or freezing to death, and she didn't regret the choice. Nothing scandalous had actually happened, unless one counted the night John had slept in the rocker downstairs because of the storm, and she didn't. But even if she never set foot in the town of Haven River Falls again—a possibility that dragged at her heart like a lead weight—she'd hate for them to think ill of her.

John's eyes darted from one of them to the other, his brows pulled together in the protective scowl she'd come to know well. "Laurie, I'd be honored if—"

She shook her head and spoke over him, unwilling to hear the rest of that sentence. It didn't take much to guess that he was about to offer to marry her, and she didn't want it. Not like that. She wouldn't let him propose out of duty or obligation or to save her reputation. If he wasn't asking out of the deepest devotion and a heart that was entirely hers, she couldn't accept it. Because that was how she loved him. She knew it now. And she wouldn't settle for a marriage that was one-sided.

"Did the Browns think that?" she asked Carlos instead.

He shook his head, shooting John a quick glance. "They were too relieved to know that you were alive and safe. And when Mrs. Harrison hinted at the tainted respectability, Miss Brown flew into a fit defending you." He smiled. "You made a good friend there, Laurie."

Laurie grinned, picturing Martha's offense on her behalf. "I know."

John made a disgruntled noise and left the table, shoving his feet into his boots and stalking outside into the rain before his coat and hat were fully on.

Laurie watched him go, her smile falling.

"He was gonna—"

"I know." She pressed her lips together. Her emotions were wrestling themselves into a tangled knot, and tears pressed against her eyes. "It was just… the wrong reason."

Carlos's expression was sympathetic. "He has all the reasons, you know."

Laurie's heart fluttered, and a tiny smile tugged at her lips. "I hope so."

Carlos followed after John, and Laurie pushed the aborted proposal from her mind. She had letters from her friends, and she intended to enjoy them. She opened Essie's first, putting off Harvey's wrath as long as she could. It was just as well that she did; Essie's first envelope contained two letters.

Dear Laurie,

I hope you're having the most splendid adventure, and I can't wait to hear all about it. Please write soon so that we know that you're safe and so that I don't die of curiosity. Nothing exciting has happened here since you left. We feel your loss every day—your cooking is infinitely superior to mine, and Beth has to work harder to keep up with orders, but more than that, you helped balance us. It was nice to have another person here so that it wasn't just us two sisters driving each other mad every day. I'm teasing (mostly), but

CHAPTER 15

we really do miss you. Of course, I hope you know that I'm wishing you all the best of luck with your rancher, but if it doesn't work out, you always have a place with us.

Next week we'll be going home to the farm to celebrate Thanksgiving with our parents. Mrs. Ellis (Robbie's mother, not Beth, obviously) invited us to join their family, but Beth and I both agreed we'd rather not spend a whole day with Harry.

In free moments—which are rare—Beth has begun sewing us both new Christmas dresses. They're deep green shot through with gold, and I've been knitting hats for each of us and for Levi. We'll look like a matching set when we attend church on Christmas Eve.

Shortly after you left, this letter arrived from Harvey. I guess he was hoping to catch you and change your mind before you headed west. I wrote to him to tell him you were already gone and to direct him where to send future letters, so you can probably expect more to come.

Missing you dearly (but so excited for you all the same),
Essie

Laurie smiled as she read her friend's words. She could hear Essie's voice in everything. A pang of homesickness hit, but it wasn't as strong as she might have expected. She missed Essie and Beth and Levi, but she didn't wish herself back with them. Which did not bode well for her if she couldn't work things out with John and had to board the train in a few days.

She opened the letter from Harvey, which was short, to the point, and horrified:

Laurie,

Are you out of your mind? What on earth could have induced you to write to a stranger, let alone agree to travel thousands of miles to meet one? I can only hope that this is a joke (one in very poor taste, and if it's Essie Martin's idea, you ought to know better than to listen to her by now). Please write immediately to reassure us. Mary's beside herself.

Harvey

Laurie couldn't help the laugh that burst out. It was almost word for word what she'd expected. What must he have thought when he got Essie's response? She drew forward the envelopes he'd sent her directly, starting with the earliest postmark.

It contained more of the same, as well as demands for a letter of assurance that she was safe and well and he needn't worry that she was dead in a ditch in some "godforsaken backwoods town." The third was like it, only with more panicked urgency. It had been sent in March, and it was even shorter than the others.

If I don't hear from you by the time I finish spring planting, I'm jumping on a train and coming to find you. And when I do, I'm hauling you home. This is absurd. You should never have left.

H.

Laurie's guilt returned at the thought of her cousin being worried about her all winter. She took out a sheet of stationery and her pen and began to write.

Dearest Harvey and Mary,

I'm so incredibly sorry to have not written to you before now. I had no idea when I came west that mail can't get to or from Haven River Falls all winter thanks to the snow. It's so different from

CHAPTER 15

Pennsylvania. It was as if I'd never truly experienced winter before. But I am writing now, and I hope you'll accept my apology. And I hope you won't jump on the next train—I'm perfectly well.

She paused then, unsure what to say next. She couldn't tell him what her next plans were because she didn't know them. Would she end up on a train? If so, this letter was redundant because she'd arrive before it would. She wanted to tell him about John and how happy she was here, but she couldn't until they'd reached an understanding. Laurie set her letter aside and picked up the last of Essie's.

Dear Laurie,

I'm nearly expiring from curiosity, you know that, don't you? Please, oh please, do write soon. What is Mr. Knowles like? Is Haven River Falls all that you hoped? I was about to fall to pieces from worry last week because we hadn't heard from you yet, but then one of our clients, Mrs. Ulrich—you remember her? She's probably the most talkative client we've had, and she loves Beth's dresses, so she comes for a new one every few months since her husband is high up in the railroad and can afford them—anyway, she was in for a fitting, and she said that her son had gone west a few years ago to run his father's railroad operations out there. She said, offhand, that no mail can get through during the winter, or if it does, it's so sporadic that she always has to wait for spring to hear from him. I hope that's true of where you are too, and that you're safe and warm. Please write to me as soon as you can. If I don't hear from you once spring arrives, I really might have a fit.

All my love,
Essie

Laurie laughed at the single sentence that made up most of the letter. It was so very Essie. She'd write to her friend soon. And she'd include all the details, even if it took her several days to write the letter. But first, sleep. It was getting late now, and morning kept coming earlier.

***

When John left the cabin, he strode to the barn, pacing the aisle as he tried to rein in his frustration. He was livid that anyone could think something so awful about Laurie, and he wished that he, like Miss Brown, could have words with Mrs. Harrison in her defense. *He* was the one who'd brought her to the ranch—not that there had been a choice—and it wasn't right that *her* reputation should suffer.

Even so, that was the way of things. She *had* spent the winter with them without another woman or a family member to chaperone. If this had happened in Boston, gossip would have spread like wildfire and she would have been ruined.

He wouldn't let that happen.

They had the same two options they'd always had—a train back east where no one knew about her winter on the ranch, or a trip to the preacher. John knew which option he preferred, hence why he'd spoken up to offer marriage. His drive to protect this amazing woman had overridden whatever reticence kept preventing him from getting the words out.

Except that *Laurie* had stopped him.

Carlos's footsteps sounded inside the barn. John didn't stop his pacing. His friend waited, watching him twist himself into tighter and tighter knots until he couldn't hold it in a moment longer.

"She wouldn't even hear me out."

Carlos just watched him. "Reckon she had a reason."

John scowled. "I only want to protect her. To make her happy. What reason could she have?" John huffed and glared at the packed dirt floor. "Other than a complete distaste for the idea of marrying me." He felt sick.

"I've seen the two of you together. It's not that."

John looked up. "Then what?"

Carlos shrugged. "I'm no expert on women, but maybe they like pretty words about love before a proposal of marriage?"

Sighing, John slumped against the door to Star's stall. The horse came over and snuffled at his shoulder. As far as proposals went, it had been a pathetic attempt. He'd been too angry at the idea of Laurie being connected to any talk of scandal to see it from that angle. She deserved so much better. But given how twisted around his thoughts and words got when he was near her, he wasn't sure how much better he could do.

Chapter 16

Laurie wasn't sure why, but the fact that morning chores felt as mundane as usual struck her as odd. The events of yesterday should have changed something fundamental, shouldn't they? John had tried to propose—possibly twice, if that had been what the rain had interrupted during their picnic—and she'd been suspected of indecent behavior. She'd received some rather desperate letters from her cousin, and they'd learned that the pass into town was open. Carlos hadn't seen any sign of Mr. Knowles, but that didn't mean anything. Her winter of safety was over.

And yet, the cows still wanted to be milked. The chickens needed to be fed. There were eggs to gather and stalls to muck and horses to care for.

She went about the tasks by habit alone, her mind darting from thought to thought. She needed to talk to John, to find out for certain what he'd been trying to say and to explain herself for last night. If she seemed forward, well, so be it. He couldn't be expected to intuit the reason she'd cut him off so rudely. But he was busy with Carlos, pitching hay to the cattle and moving the horses to the paddock so their stalls could be cleaned. She was beginning to despair of ever getting him alone when he appeared at the open door of Milky Way's stall where she was

CHAPTER 16

spreading clean hay. She leaned on the pitchfork as she looked up at him. Sudden shyness overtook her. Anything she'd been hoping to say disappeared from her mind when faced with the earnest expression in those blue-green eyes.

He held his gloves in one hand, and he rubbed the back of his neck with the other. "Can we... can we talk later?"

Laurie nodded, finding her voice. "I'm going to start planting in the greenhouse when I'm done with this."

He held her gaze for a second, then slapped his gloves against his other hand and nodded. "I'll find you."

Nerves and happiness swirled through her. Whatever happened in the coming conversation, she was looking forward a few minutes alone with John.

Laurie hurried through the rest of her chores, dropping off the eggs and milk at the cabin and grabbing the jar of seeds from the table. It was turning into a beautiful spring day with the bluest sky Laurie could remember seeing. The glass of the greenhouse only amplified the sun's warmth, and she removed her coat and hung it on a nail by the door. She had to put it back on a moment later when she realized that she had no labels to show what she'd planted and had to go back inside to get her pen and paper. Then she had to search through the storage room in the barn for stakes she could use. She didn't find any, but she did find a hammer and a handful of nails, so she brought those along to tack the labels to the wooden framework of the greenhouse walls.

"No good comes of haste and distraction," she muttered to herself as she shucked her coat again. Her mother used to say that to her as a child when she rushed and left chores half done. Apparently, she hadn't outgrown the tendency. She took a deep breath and let it out slowly, allowing her gaze to roam the small space.

She'd mentally laid out the garden the other day when she'd seen what seeds they had available. She spread out the paper packets on the shelf accordingly, realizing that the seeds Carlos had bought in town hadn't been added to the jar. Laurie shrugged and made a mental note to ask John about them when he came in later; she'd already wasted enough time going from building to building. She had enough seeds to keep her busy for a while as it was.

Laurie hadn't been lying when she'd told John how much she loved the greenhouse. She basked in the light and warmth and relished the feel of dirt beneath her fingers as she loosened the soil and lovingly planted each seed. She tore her sheet of paper into small sections, wrote labels, and nailed them to the nearest bit of wood. Gardening was soothing, and Laurie found her mind calming, quieting, relaxing into the activity.

She was halfway along the bed beneath the shelf when she heard the door creak open. She smiled and, without looking up, opened her mouth to tell John that they'd need more carrot seeds because she'd just used the last. But another voice spoke before she did.

"So this is where you've been hiding."

A tall shadow blocked the sun, sending a shiver through her. Laurie gasped and jerked her head up to see Mr. Knowles towering over her. Before she could react, he grabbed her arm and roughly hauled her to her feet.

"Let me go!" She tried to jerk her arm away, but his fingers gripped like a vise.

He leaned in close, too close. His pungent breath reeked of alcohol, and she cringed away. "Not this time."

"How did you find me?"

CHAPTER 16

"Word travels fast in such a small town. You got some nerve running out on me like that. But I get what I want."

"No," Laurie said, her voice rising in fear. "No! I won't marry you. I want nothing to do with you."

"Oh, I ain't talking marriage anymore, you little tart. You had your chance."

Laurie's stomach lurched, and bile rose in her throat. She darted her gaze around, searching for anything she could use as a weapon. The hammer and nails lay on the shelf. The hammer was too far for her to reach, but if she could just grab a nail…. She lunged, her fingers closing over the small metal spike. Whirling, she jabbed it into the fleshy part of his hand between his thumb and index finger.

Mr. Knowles snatched his hand away, but his other hand shot out faster than Laurie could move, catching her again as he cursed her roundly. She wished she could unhear the poisonous words. His bleeding hand came around and pried the nail from her fingers, despite how hard she fought. Before she knew it, he had her by both wrists and was towing her toward the door. If they were outside, maybe she could scream loud enough to alert John and Carlos. But would they even hear her? The ranch was huge, and she had no idea how far out they'd ridden this morning. If Mr. Knowles got her out of the greenhouse, he could drag her to his horse and carry her off with nobody the wiser.

***

John had lain awake all night thinking about how he'd propose to Laurie. By dawn, he thought he'd figured out the right words to say how he felt. He just hoped he'd be able to remember them when she was right there. Something about this girl made him go dopey and giddy, things he'd never experienced before.

It had taken the whole morning for him to work up the courage to ask her to talk. Somehow, each of his previous failed attempts had ratcheted up the pressure, weighing heavily on his shoulders. He finally stopped by the stall where she was working because if he didn't get the words out soon, the suspense would physically kill him.

Once they'd agreed to talk later in the greenhouse, John was good for nothing. He continued to work with Carlos, getting tasks done, but he was a mess of nerves and excitement and dread and hope, and several times his friend had to shout at him to get his attention.

"Sorry," he muttered when this happened again.

"Just go talk to her, boss. Get it over with."

"Not yet," John said, glancing in the direction of the cabin, which was hidden beyond the barn. "We'll check the calving mothers and then I'll go."

When they rode up to the paddock where the mother cows who were near to giving birth were still secluded, something was wrong. The energy was different. It didn't take long to find the source: one of the mothers was in active labor. Together they examined her, determining that she was in good shape and could probably manage without intervention. Carlos stayed to keep an eye on her, while John ran for the cabin. With how much Laurie doted on Orion and Ursa, he could only imagine how magical she'd find an actual birth. He grinned, nerves forgotten as he pictured her delighted smile.

He slowed to a stop as he rounded the corner of the barn. A horse stood ground tied in the middle of the yard. A strange horse with a poorly kept saddle, standing in the mud without

CHAPTER 16

any grass to graze on nearby.

A chill swept through him, and he was sprinting into the barn for his rifle before his conscious mind caught up. Laurie was alone in the greenhouse while a stranger roamed the ranch. And John had a sickening feeling that he knew who it was.

***

Laurie dug her heels into the packed dirt of the narrow pathway, throwing all her weight against Mr. Knowles's pull on her wrists. "No!" she shrieked. "I won't go. You can't do this." She struggled and tried to twist her arms from his grip, but he held her so tightly that she knew she'd have bruises. She kicked at his shins with the solid heel of her boot, and he shouted and swore. Then he released one hand just long enough to backhand her across the face.

Laurie cried out and would have fallen if he hadn't had such a firm grip on her other arm. Her vision went funny for a minute, and her head spun, shaking her up enough that she couldn't make use of her free arm before he caught it again.

"You'll learn to show some respect," Mr. Knowles snarled.

She tried to regain her balance enough to land another kick but the metallic click of a cocked rifle caused them both to freeze.

"Take your hands off her."

John's welcome voice washed over her like a river of sunlight. Mr. Knowles turned slightly to look over his shoulder, giving Laurie a view of the rancher standing in the open doorway, glaring down the barrel of a rifle aimed directly at Mr. Knowles's heart.

"You gonna shoot?" The cowboy sneered.

"Wouldn't be opposed to it." John's voice was colder than a snowstorm, and his blue-green eyes held an icy chill. "Hands off her."

"You ain't got no right to her," Mr. Knowles snarled. "She's *mine*. *I* sent for her; she came for *me*."

"She doesn't belong to you or me or anyone else. She belongs to her own self." John's eyes flickered to Laurie for the briefest second. "Now I'm losing patience, and my trigger finger's itchy. Take your hands off her."

Todd Knowles released Laurie's wrists with a shove that sent her stumbling against the wooden shelf. Her ribs ached at the contact, but she ignored it, reaching for the hammer and gripping it firmly. Mr. Knowles shot her a glower, but he lifted his hands to shoulder level where John could see them.

"Get out of there." John stepped back slowly, keeping the gun trained on the filthy cowboy as he stalked from the greenhouse.

Laurie stood frozen where she was, clutching her makeshift weapon tightly as she watched them leave.

***

Fire and fury burned through John, but his hands were steady as he held the rifle fixed on Knowles. He kept the man moving, keeping pace with him until he reached his horse.

"If you touch her again," he warned in a low, fierce growl, "or if you so much as set foot on my property, you'll be no more than a lead-riddled carcass."

He stood where he was, rifle at the ready, until Knowles was in the saddle and out of sight on the track back toward town. Lowering the gun, John took a deep breath. He'd never shot a man before, never even considered it, but today he'd have done

CHAPTER 16

it willingly. No man would hurt Laurie without regretting it.

He turned on his heel and raced back to the greenhouse. Laurie hadn't moved from where she'd fallen against the shelf, the hammer clenched in one fist. Her eyes were wide and fearful, and her whole body shook.

"Sweetheart?" he murmured, leaning the gun against the wall and stepping slowly and cautiously toward her.

"John." Her whimper broke his heart, and he gently took her in his arms. She buried her face against his neck and sobbed into his collar. They stayed there for a long time, until the tremors stopped and the sobs faded to weak sniffles. John lowered one arm to stroke her hand, coaxing her to release the hammer. She dropped it to the ground and, freed of its weight, slipped her hands into the open front of his jacket and around his waist.

He'd never let her go. He couldn't. Just the thought that he could have lost her this morning made him hold her even closer. But he hadn't been lying when he'd said she belonged to only herself. The choice was hers, and she deserved to make it. He cleared his throat.

"If you want, I'll saddle a pair of horses right this minute to take you to the train station. I wouldn't blame you, and I stand by my promise to keep you safe. But…" His voice caught. "Maybe instead you could stick around… and marry me."

Those weren't the words he'd rehearsed all night, and he kicked himself for forgetting them.

"Shoot, I don't know how to say these things," he muttered. "I've never felt like this about anyone before."

Laurie raised her head. "John…"

Her warm brown eyes were red rimmed, and tears streaked her cheeks. He couldn't breathe, couldn't think beyond the desire to kiss away those salty trails. With one hand, he gently pressed her head back down to his shoulder, cradling it there as he kissed her temple.

"Stay right there," he said. "I can't get through this if you're looking at me." She made a noise of protest, and he chuckled. "Your eyes… your mouth… I forget how to think. I love you, Laurie. I've been falling for you since that first day. You could have stayed in the cabin and never done a lick of work all winter, and I wouldn't have minded—I'd've just worshipped you from afar." He grinned as he remembered his first look at her without her hat and scarf hiding her face and hair. She'd stunned him for sure. "But then you jumped in and got your hands dirty, which only made me fall harder. You've made this place feel more like home than it ever has, even when George was around. I never saw it coming. And I can't help dreaming about what our forever could look like. I'll do whatever you want, sweetheart, even if it means saying goodbye, but I want you to stay—so badly it hurts."

There was a pause, then Laurie said, "Can I lift my head now?"

John chuckled and stroked his hand down her silky hair before wrapping that arm back around her shoulders. "Yep, sorry. It just feels so right to hold you like this."

Even with the signs of her ordeal, Laurie was beautiful as she beamed up at him. "I agree."

John's heart soared. "Really?"

She nodded.

"Then will you marry me?"

She nodded again, eyes shining.

John wasted no time doing what he'd been dreaming of for months. He captured her mouth with his, his pulse skyrocketing as she fervently kissed him back. His mind felt dopier than ever when they finally broke the kiss. Laurie looked dazed as she grinned up at him.

"That was even better than I thought." John couldn't help but agree with her. "I think that needs to happen again every day for the rest of our lives. Is that how you envisioned our future? Because that's how I've imagined it."

"You've imagined it too?"

"Every day." John couldn't stop smiling. "And what do you see? Besides kissing, which I intend to do as often as you'll let me."

She laughed and tilted her head up to present her lips for another kiss right then. He obliged.

Pulling back just an inch, Laurie whispered, "I see home. You, John Newcomb, are where I belong. And I never want to leave."

Chapter 17

Laurie was walking on air. Other than some soreness that would turn into bruising later, Mr. Knowles and his attack were all but forgotten. John had rescued her; he loved her; she could trust his promise to protect her.

After several more minutes of exploratory kisses ranging from sweet to intense, John eventually seemed to recall why he'd been coming out to find her in the first place. They walked hand in hand to the pasture, where the newborn calf had already arrived and was being licked clean by its mother.

"There you are." Carlos shook his head in mock exasperation, but his eyes gleamed and a smirk curled his lips as he saw their clasped hands. "Thought you were coming right back."

"We got held up," John said. "It's a longer story than you'd think, but I'll tell you later. Is there a stall ready for them?"

"Not yet. I'll get mama cleaned up awhile. She's been lying in the mud and needs a bit of a wash before this little guy nurses. Got a name for him, Laurie?"

Laurie couldn't help grinning at the messy, gangly, disoriented little creature. "I'll have to think on it," she said.

"You don't need to stick to stars and such," John murmured, squeezing her hand lightly. "This ranch is yours too now, or will be as soon as I can make it so. You can choose whatever

CHAPTER 17

names you like."

Laurie leaned her head against his shoulder, touched by his sweetness. "What about Sawyer?" she asked, thinking of Pa's favorite book.

John exchanged a look with Carlos and nodded. "Sawyer it is. Now let's go get that stall ready for them." He tugged her toward the barn. "They won't need to stay indoors as long as Orion and Polaris—we'll let them out on the range when the herd goes."

There was only one empty stall left, and it didn't take long to lay out a bed of hay. They returned to the pasture with blankets, and Laurie watched as the men wrapped up the newborn and draped him over Crescent's saddle. Carlos rode with the calf to the barn, while John followed with the mama on a lead rope. As long as they were trailing her calf, she was cooperative, but Laurie thought she might get belligerent if she was kept from her baby too long.

Once the animals were settled, the three of them leaned against the stall door to watch them.

"So, when are you getting hitched?" Carlos asked.

"How does tomorrow sound?"

Laurie looked up at John in surprise. Harvey and Mary had planned their wedding months in advance, and there had been a big potluck and dancing in the afternoon. But when she thought about it, neither she nor John had any family here, and she could count their close friends on one hand.

He must have seen her eyes widen. He smiled and leaned in. "I want to give you the protection of my name as soon as possible." A mischievous glint shone in his eye as he added, "Among other reasons."

Laurie's cheeks burned, and her stomach swooped. She

liked the sound of "other reasons." She also appreciated his protectiveness more now than she ever had. It showed how much he cared about her, and he wasn't wrong: she'd be safer and her reputation more secure once they were legally wed.

"You don't mind if it's not a big event?" she asked. Surely the Boston weddings he'd grown up with were fancy affairs.

"I don't mind at all. As long as it's you, me, and the preacher, I'm happy." His eyes were warm and adoring, and Laurie could have drowned in them. "I'd marry you today if I thought we could get to and from town in time."

Laurie couldn't say a word, her heart was so full.

"Tomorrow, then?" Carlos's voice broke into the moment. Laurie had almost forgotten he was standing nearby. She tore her eyes from John's.

"Tomorrow," she agreed. "You'll come, won't you?"

Carlos grinned. "Wouldn't miss it."

***

Before sunrise the next morning, Laurie milked Andie and Cass and cared for the chickens while the men handled the cattle and horses. John packed up his things from the stall he and Carlos had been sleeping in and carried them back to the cabin. Laurie's cheeks flushed at the knowledge that he'd be staying in the cabin with her from this night on, and she leaned her head against Andie's warm side until the embarrassment passed.

When her chores were done, she put on her Sunday dress, which she'd only worn a few times to church while staying at th boarding house. It felt prim and stiff after spending the whole winter in ordinary, work-day dresses. But a woman

CHAPTER 17

wore her best on her wedding day. She dug Mama's ring from the bottom of her carpetbag and slipped it into her pocket, along with the letter to Harvey that she'd finished last night.

The horses were saddled and ready in the yard when she stepped outside and latched the door. She and the two men mounted up and rode to town together as the sun rose. The trip took less time than it had in Mr. Harrison's wagon when she'd arrived, and much less than when she'd walked on the morning of her escape. Laurie felt like she'd barely gotten comfortable in Moonbeam's saddle before they were cresting the pass and easing down the switchbacks on the other side. Of course, that was probably all in her head—excitement, nerves, and good company could make actual time speed by.

They pulled up in front of the livery stable, a building Laurie hadn't been to before. Dismounting, they passed their reins to a young stable hand, the son of the livery's owner.

The boarding house was only a stone's throw away, but Laurie felt exposed and on edge. Moonbeam had given her courage, both by placing her higher than the tallest cowboy and promising a quick escape should she need it. Now, standing on her own two feet, she darted her eyes up and down the street and over her shoulder, afraid a tall, dark shadow would fall on her again.

John stepped close beside her and silently took her hand and guided it through the crook of his arm, tucking her close to his side. As they walked out of the livery yard, Carlos fell in with them, keeping half a step behind on Laurie's other side. The relief of knowing that he had her back and that John would move heaven and earth to protect her eased her shallow breathing. She didn't relax until they were on the doorstep of the boarding house, however.

John knocked, then brought his hand to cover Laurie's, causing a sizzle of delight to shoot up her arm. Mrs. Brown pulled the door open with a pleasant smile, which grew into an expression of pure joy when her gaze fell on them.

"You're here! And safe!" She pulled Laurie into a tight embrace. "We were so worried about you, dear—why didn't you tell us where you were going? You disappeared so suddenly, we didn't know…" Her words trailed off, and Laurie wasn't surprised when she saw tears brimming in the woman's eyes.

"I'm sorry," she said. "I didn't know what else to do. But you can see, I'm safe, and John—Mr. Newcomb—and I are getting married today."

That started off a whole new ruckus of crying, cheering, and laughing. All three of them were bustled inside, where Martha joined her mother's enthusiasm. After a minute or two, John cleared his throat. Laurie was afraid the ladies' bubbly giddiness had made him uncomfortable, but he was grinning ear to ear.

"Any chance your husband could give me a shave and a trim before we head to the church?"

"Of course, of course!" Mrs. Brown led him away, calling for her husband as she went.

"May I dress your hair, Laurie?" Martha asked eagerly. "It's not every day your friend gets married." Laurie heard her unspoken words: especially not here in Haven River Falls where women were so badly outnumbered. She remembered sitting in the parlor with Martha when she'd first arrived and letting the younger girl comb her hair.

"That would be so sweet," she said, perching on the sofa and turning a little sideways so that Martha could reach her hair. It hung over her shoulder in its usual braid, which Martha soon loosed.

"Would you give us a moment, Mr. Vasquez?" Martha said primly with an arch smile at the cowboy. "This is girl time. Besides, you could do with a haircut yourself."

Laurie stifled a giggle at the teasing. If she wasn't mistaken, her friend was trying to flirt with Carlos.

"Sorry, Miss Brown, but I'm honor bound to stay. Boss made me promise to stick close to La—Miss Kerstetter whenever he couldn't."

Laurie could tell from his expression that John had filled him in about Mr. Knowles. Martha must have noticed something in his expression too because she looked back and forth between them with a furrowed brow.

"Why would he do that? Did something happen?" she asked.

Laurie nodded. She didn't wish to relive what had happened, but she wanted her young friend to know and to be on her guard. If she didn't go into detail, she could probably get through it. "You fix my hair while I tell you about it. And Mr. Vasquez can stay, since he already knows."

So while Martha plied brush and comb and braided ribbons into Laurie's hair, pinning it all in a complex knot, Laurie told her about Mr. Knowles's unexpected and definitely unwelcome visit to the ranch the day before.

Martha's eyes were practically bugging out of her head by the time Laurie finished the abbreviated version of the story, and her hands had frozen halfway through placing a hairpin.

"How awful!" she gasped. "But how romantic that Mr. Newcomb came to your rescue." She sighed dreamily, and Laurie noticed that Carlos's gaze held unwaveringly on her friend.

"I've never been happier to see anyone in my life," Laurie

agreed with a shiver.

Martha's hands busied themselves at the task again. She had just placed the last pin and given it a triumphant pat when footsteps sounded from the doorway. Laurie glanced up, and her breath caught. John stood there, looking like he had when she'd met him in November, clean-shaven and short-haired. In his fresh Sunday clothes, he looked less rugged than she had gotten used to but still masculine and appealing and... *mmm*. Warmth pooled in Laurie's belly, and she didn't miss the way his eyes locked onto her.

Carlos left the room to get his own haircut, and Martha took away her hairdressing supplies and promised to bring back tea and cakes. John sat on the couch with Laurie, taking her hand in his. She scooted closer so that her arm and thigh were pressed against his.

He cleared his throat. "Are you sure you don't want a big, fancy wedding? Miss Brown gave you the right hairstyle for one."

Laurie laughed. "I'm sure. I couldn't deny her the opportunity. But," she tipped her head to look up at him through her lashes, "I might need your help to take it all out later."

A low sound rumbled through his chest as his eyes darkened, sending a delicious shiver through her. "I've been wanting to run my hands through your hair for *months*," he groaned.

Laurie stretched up to kiss his smooth cheek, sitting back as Martha reentered the room. They made small talk for several minutes until Carlos returned, looking tidy and even a little dashing with his short hair and clean shave. Laurie's eyes widened, and she laughed. "I've never seen you without a beard!"

Carlos ran a hand over his jaw and colored slightly. "It's a rare enough sight." He gave her a rueful grin.

"He does clean up well, doesn't he?" Martha tilted her head to consider him appraisingly.

"Quite well," John said, getting to his feet and offering Laurie his hand to help her up. "Now that we're all presentable, let's get to the church."

Chapter 18

Laurie invited Mrs. Brown and Martha to come with them and witness the wedding, grateful to have even this small handful of friends with them. Walking through town wasn't nearly as frightening now that she was surrounded by a group of people. Mr. Knowles wouldn't dare try anything.

The church was a boxy structure, with one open room on the first floor and a second-story apartment where the preacher lived. There were only two wooden benches in the church room and a rough wooden cross on the wall opposite the door. Laurie had sat on the front bench with Martha and her mother during the few Sundays she'd attended in the fall. Now the two ladies sat while Carlos ran up the outside stairs to knock on the preacher's door.

Laurie hung back near the entrance of the church with John. She reached one hand into her pocket, pulled out the ring, and held it out to him, admiring how the sunlight streaming through the open door gleamed on the gold band and made the small ruby glow. "This was my mother's ring," she said, her eyes darting to his and back to the glittering stone. Memories swirled through her, of her mother's capable hands hulling strawberries to preserve, the stone in her ring matching the

CHAPTER 18

bright berries. Of her father, taking Mama's hand and kissing the knuckle above the ring, as obviously smitten with his wife as he had been the day he'd married her. Of Mrs. Martin, Beth and Essie's mother, coming to Laurie after the women had helped prepare Mama's body for the funeral and pressing the ring silently into Laurie's hand. She swallowed hard and blinked back tears.

John's strong fingers curled around hers. "I'm honored to be the man who gets to put this ring on your finger," he whispered, leaning in so that their foreheads were touching. "You are such an incredible woman, sweetheart—your parents would be very proud."

He reached up to brush away the single tear that escaped down her cheek.

Two sets of heavy treads sounded on the wooden stairs outside, and John pulled back just a little, slipping the ring from Laurie's grasp as Carlos and the minister, Reverend Oliver appeared. Reverend Oliver was a plump middle-aged man with dark hair going silver at the temples. He wore wire-rimmed spectacles and smiled warmly when he saw them. Laurie had liked him from the first—he had a way of making everyone feel welcome, cared for, and appreciated with only a smile and a word or two.

He greeted them both with a handshake. "It's not every day I get to preside over a wedding. Thank you for the opportunity."

"Thank *you*," John said, shooting a grin at Laurie.

After a few more words, Reverend Oliver took his place at the front of the church, and Carlos sat on the bench beside the Browns. Laurie took John's arm, and they walked together to stand before the preacher. The ceremony was short and simple, just a verse of scripture and the exchanging of vows.

John slipped Mama's ring onto Laurie's finger and kissed her to cheers and whistles from their tiny audience.

Everyone offered congratulations, and Martha took Laurie's hand to admire the ring. "I hope you're not riding back to the ranch right away," she said after a minute. "It's been so long. Do you… I don't know, do you have any errands we could run? Anything you need at the mercantile? I know Mr. Vasquez was just here…"

Laurie squeezed her hand. "As a matter of fact, I have a letter to take to the mercantile," she said. "And there were some seeds I forgot to write on the last shopping list." She shivered as she remembered the day before in the greenhouse. She never had gotten around to telling John about the carrot seeds, and half the beds were still waiting to be planted.

"Perfect," Martha beamed. "We'll go together."

Mrs. Brown excused herself to prepare luncheon at the boarding house, inviting them all to come eat before they set off.

Laurie, Martha, and the two men said goodbye to Reverend Oliver and walked in the direction of the mercantile. Laurie clung to John's arm again, but this time it was because she simply wanted to be as close as possible to her new husband, not because she was afraid of anyone else in town. Carlos and Martha fell in beside each other, walking a short way ahead and talking like old friends.

Halfway through town, they passed the sheriff's office, and John hesitated.

"I want to tell Sheriff Hill about…" He trailed off, frowning, but he didn't need to finish the sentence for Laurie to know what he meant.

"Do I need to come?" It had been bad enough telling Martha

CHAPTER 18

a short version of the story. Telling a stranger would be more uncomfortable, and the sheriff would want details.

"Not if you don't want to." He leaned in and kissed her forehead. "Stick with Carlos and wait for me at the mercantile."

Laurie nodded and gave his arm a final squeeze before letting go. She hurried to catch up to her friends as he knocked on the sheriff's door.

Laurie hadn't been to the mercantile in months, and her attention was caught by the display window. Beautiful hand-carved wooden animals played a game of hide and seek around mixing bowls, tools, and bolts of cloth. She admired a dog, a horse, a cat, and a pig, then forced her feet to move her toward the door that Carlos held open. Martha had already gone inside.

"I'm coming," Laurie said, catching the handle of the door as Carlos stepped halfway through the doorway to respond to something Martha had said. But as she moved to follow, Laurie saw the little wooden goat. It was a perfect replica of the goats she'd had on the farm and small enough to fit in her palm. The lines of the carving captured the goat's hair perfectly, and its expression reminded her so forcibly of Buttercup, one of the most troublesome kids she'd ever raised, that she had to laugh. She studied the goat for another moment, determined to ask how much it cost.

But before she could tug on the door handle and go inside, an unwelcome voice spoke from nearby.

"You're awful brazen to come into town after you shacked up with another man when you were promised to me."

Laurie gasped and turned to face Mr. Knowles, keeping her grip on the door handle. The cowboy leaned against the corner of the building, half hidden by shadow. Only a few paces separated them.

"Nothing was promised," Laurie spat, fear and anger and disgust writhing in her stomach. "And I did nothing of the sort."

"Of course you did, you filthy hussy." He sneered, his venomous words matching his hateful glare. He prowled a step toward her.

"No one speaks to my wife like that."

Laurie nearly melted with relief as John approached. He stopped beside her, one hand coming to rest reassuringly against her low back. The air around him seemed to ripple with fury. Every muscle in him was tensed for a fight, and his free hand hovered over the pistol holstered at his hip.

"I ain't on your land," Mr. Knowles growled with a significant look at the pistol. "And I ain't touchin' her. I wouldn't want to dirty myself with such a faithless, four-flushing doxy."

John seemed to forget about the gun as he stepped forward and cocked his fist back.

"Is there a problem, fellas?"

Another voice broke into the moment, making John pause instead of throwing the first punch, though he didn't once take his eyes off Mr. Knowles.

Laurie glanced away from the action for only a moment to see that the newcomer was Deputy Cooper, his sole hand resting ominously on his own pistol. He narrowed his eyes at the two men, then looked at Laurie.

"You alright, ma'am?"

Laurie took a shaky breath. "I'm fine," she said, less evenly than she wished. "But I'm glad you're here, deputy."

"I stopped by the office to report this man to the sheriff," John said, lowering his fist and stepping back to Laurie's side, still keeping the cowboy in his sights, "but he was out."

"I'll hear your report," Deputy Cooper said. His normally friendly demeanor was stern and businesslike. "Do I need to lock him in the cell first?"

Laurie didn't know what to say—she would have felt much safer if he'd been locked away, but he hadn't actually done anything but spew toxic words today. Before either she or John could reply, however, the snake turned on his heel and disappeared between buildings.

John slid his arm around Laurie's waist and pulled her close to his side. She didn't realize until that moment that she was trembling or that her knuckles had gone white with how tightly she was grasping the door handle. She let go and leaned into her new husband, letting his strength bolster her.

"I've got you, sweetheart," he whispered.

"Do you need to sit for a minute, Miss Kerstetter?"

"Mrs. Newcomb," Laurie murmured, turning to rest her forehead against John's shoulder for a moment. She closed her eyes and took a deep breath, letting his scent of horses and hard work and the great outdoors fill her lungs. She raised her head and looked at Deputy Cooper. "I'm Mrs. Newcomb now. We just came from the church."

"Congratulations to you both." The deputy's stern expression melted into a grin. "Is now a good time to talk at the office?"

"Can we take a minute in here first?" Laurie gestured to the door of the mercantile. "I have a letter to mail, and Martha—"

John stiffened, as if he'd forgotten where they were and what they'd been doing before the scuffle broke out. His arm tightened around her waist. "What were you doing outside by yourself? Where's Carlos?"

"I was just following them inside when I saw the goat in the window and got distracted." Both men looked surprised and alarmed until she pointed to the small wooden figure. "It looks so much like one I raised a few years ago."

John shook his head slowly. It had been a while since he'd looked like she utterly baffled him, but the expression was back. He looked adorable when he was confused, and Laurie decided she'd try to leave him bewildered at least once a week just for that.

Deputy Cooper chuckled. "All's well that ends well, I guess. You come find me at the office when you're done here."

The two men shook hands, then John opened the mercantile door for her. He let go of her waist so that she could go through the door first, his hand finding hers as they stepped out of the bright sun. Laurie's eyes were still adjusting to the dim interior when John tugged her by the hand down a side aisle and between two tall shelves that shielded them from other shop patrons. He dropped her hand, using one arm at her waist to pull her close and the other to support her neck as he kissed her, hard. It didn't last long—not nearly long enough, in Laurie's opinion—but they were both breathless when he broke the kiss.

"No more scaring me like that," he grumbled, kissing her forehead, her cheek, her nose. "You're not allowed out of my sight until I've taught you to shoot a six-gun. We'll practice with the shotgun too."

Laurie huffed a surprised laugh. "Won't do me much good if I don't have one on me."

"You're a western woman now, Mrs. Newcomb." John punctuated this statement with a firm kiss to the lips as he called her by her new name. "We'll talk to Harrison about getting you your own Colt." One more kiss, and he released her, offering his arm. When she took it, he tugged her closer so that their shoulders brushed. "And we'll buy you that goat from the window, too. Once you're settled in, we can get you some real goats if you want."

Laurie's heart swelled, and she couldn't believe how her life had changed in the last year. She'd lost her father and her sense of belonging last spring, but she'd found the home her heart longed for with this sweet, strong, wonderful man.

***

Dearest Essie,

I'm so sorry you've had to wait such a long time for a letter. Mrs. Ulrich was absolutely right—we've had no mail coming or going for the whole winter. I had no idea, and I felt awful about leaving you in suspense once I found out. But I'm writing now, and I hope you'll forgive the wait.

I also hope you'll ship my trunks out when you get the chance. I never expected when I boarded the train that I'd be limited to what I'd packed into one bag for months!

Now for the biggest news: I'm married. And before you get yourself in a tizzy because you're just now hearing about it, the wedding was only two days ago. It's going to take me a week or more to write a satisfactorily detailed letter, but I did start it right away.

My husband's name is John Newcomb. He owns a cattle ranch north of Haven River Falls with nearly four hundred head. Carlos Vasquez is the only full-time ranch hand, but they've hired on some seasonal help. They always do for the cattle drives and the branding, but John's planning to build a bedroom onto the cabin, and he'll need extra help for that too. The loft is where we sleep now, but John declares he won't let me climb the ladder to the loft once I'm in the family way, and I believe him. He'll bring the mattress down and put it right in the middle of the kitchen before he lets me do anything he thinks is dangerous. Ridiculous man.

I wish I could sit with you by the willows behind the old schoolhouse again and giggle over our imaginary romances like we used to. Only this time, my romance is real. I'm still pinching myself. John's the sweetest, most thoughtful man—he respects me and listens to me and treats me like the best thing that ever happened to him. Which is perfect, since he's the best thing that ever happened to me.

We met in November when he saved my life. But that's not the beginning of the story. I should start farther back, when I got to Haven River Falls and met Mr. Knowles, who was not at all what he made himself out to be. You'll never believe this story....

***

***

Thank you for reading Haven River Rescue! *I hope you enjoyed it as much as I did. If you loved it, please leave a review on Amazon to help another reader find a book they'll love.*

It means so much to me that you've taken the time to experience Haven River Falls. If you want to know more about the town's founding, the story is told in Haven River Beginning, *a short prequel romance set in 1850 on the Oregon Trail. You can find it for free at elizaprokopovits.com/christie-williams.*

And read Essie and Matt's story in Haven River Surprise, *coming January 14, 2025.*

Happy reading!

Christie

Milton Keynes UK
Ingram Content Group UK Ltd.
UKHW020738071024
449371UK00014B/938